AFRICAN WRITERS SERIES   FOUNDING EDITOR Chinua Achebe

Mongo Beti

MISSION TO KALA

Translated from the French by

Peter Green

HEINEMANN
LONDON · IBADAN · NAIROBI

Heinemann Educational Books Ltd
22 Bedford Square, London WC1B 3HH
P.M.B. 5205 Ibadan · P.O. Box 45314 Nairobi
EDINBURGH MELBOURNE AUCKLAND
HONG KONG SINGAPORE KUALA LUMPUR NEW DELHI
KINGSTON PORT OF SPAIN
Heinemann Educational Books Inc.
4 Front Street, Exeter, New Hampshire 03833, USA

ISBN 0 435 90013 7

First published in French as
Mission Terminée 1957
© Editions Corréa, Buchet-Chastel, 1957
This translation © Frederick Muller Ltd, 1958
First published 1958

First published in *African Writers Series* 1964
Reprinted 1966, 1968, 1969 (twice), 1970,
1971, 1972, 1974, 1977, 1979, 1980, 1982

Made and printed in Great Britain by
Richard Clay (The Chaucer Press) Ltd,
Bungay, Suffolk

PROLOGUE

Why do the events which form this story plague me so? The memory of them pours back into my mind again and again, like a sea tide. I may be depressed or cheerful: it makes no difference. The impulse absorbs every mood: romantic enthusiasm, nostalgia, indifference, the lot. Why?

There's nothing I can do about it. All my other memories, exposed to the scorching light of maturity, break up, melt, and blur into nothing, like a block of ice left out in the sun. But this adolescent adventure refuses to vanish. With lonely and heroic obstinacy it sticks in my mind, filling the gaps left by my lost youth. It has become an all-possessive obsession.

What is the reason? Has it some special significance which I have failed to unravel? I simply don't know.

But you, my friend, may see more clearly. You have travelled the same road as I, and made an almost identical journey up a very similar river. Your naked feet have trodden the same dusty laterite. Surely this fragment – already tattered and worn – of our younger days, this rusty, worm-eaten signpost on the road we both knew, will stir some familiar echo in your mind: the long-forgotten voice of a childhood friend, or a mother's favourite fairy-tale, heard again years after her death?

CHAPTER ONE

In which the reader will learn of the eventful journey that forms an alarming prelude to our hero's adventures during his vacations ; and also hear about certain matrimonial difficulties, as a result of which one Niam (a most untrustworthy person) without shame or scruple, sends a young boy hardly out of his cradle on a dangerous expedition into unknown and possibly hostile territory.

EVERY time I recall this little adventure of mine, I feel a sudden unpleasant urge to turn back the clock and begin it all over again. It was in July, if you remember, and I (together with several others of my class, whose names I now forget) had just failed the oral in my *baccalauréat* exams. I am sure you have not forgotten the formula I discovered after this set-back to counter anyone who asked me how I had done: it always amused you. 'Oh, I was ploughed – in the best tradition,' I would say. The words *in the best tradition* always came out in a faintly assertive tone: they served as a kind of alibi, and relieved both my questioner and myself of the need to go through all the misfortunes that had led up to this particular failure. (I have a nasty feeling that, as a result, I have become a kind of professional failure; but that is another story.)

Do you remember how cheerful we all were as we left the Native School the day after that solemn prize-giving? In fact, I found it difficult to disguise my bitterness from you. It was lucky that we had friends with us – such as that extraordinary chap Daniel – whose irrepressible wit and high spirits took me out of myself, and stopped me doing what the romantic poets would describe as 'meditating on my sad destiny'. Do you remember how Daniel always used to say that *his* ancestors weren't Gauls but Bantus, and had stayed Bantus ever since? And his prediction that wherever there was a Negro, there would always be some European colonial to kick his backside?

It was fairly late in the morning when we separated, and I boarded my bus alone. Usually the forty-mile trip from Ongola to my village lasted about three hours. On this occasion it took considerably longer.

I settled down on the wooden bench and made a good resolution to pass the journey profitably. I would not merely sit in unhappy contemplation of my misfortune (a condition to which I was decidedly prone). No. There were three months of vacation at my disposal; I would spend my time working out the best way in which to spread my revision work over them, in readiness for the coming academic year.

Unfortunately, my evil genius had decided to give me no respite. I was to be forced to admit his absolute powers over me. The vibrations of the bus-engine seemed to have burst the sky, as though it were some gigantic water-bottle: rain poured down in floods, drumming angrily on the roof, never letting up, the kind of deluge which gives the impression of driving your hut a little more firmly into the earth foundations. The bus (a kind of long hut on wheels) bogged itself down in the mud at every opportunity. The owner-driver, a Greek, would get out in in the rain, followed a little reluctantly by his two Negro employees. Off they would go into the bush, and come back a few moments later with armfuls of branches and foliage. These they spread in front of the tyres to stop the bus digging itself in.

This trick worked four times in succession. The fifth time we came within an inch of tragedy. The bus was vainly trying to climb a steep hill, and the rain was pouring down in torrents. Far from assisting us, the branches-and-leaves operation nearly produced a catastrophe. Instead of going forward, the bus, like a frantic cow, slewed sideways across the road, its bonnet hanging over the very edge of a precipice. It was a sheer drop,

2

and if we had slid into the ravine we shouldn't have had a chance of surviving. Luckily, the old bus snorted, pawed the ground a bit, and stayed put. The Greek driver switched off his engine and began to swear to himself.

'*Blast!*' he said, and then: 'Ah Christ, the old whore!' A pregnant pause. 'Christ, the old bastard!'

He then launched into an extraordinary flood of polyglot obscenity, compounded of French, Italian, Greek, and English which it would be impossible to transcribe even with the aid of phonetic orthography. As poor Kritikos spat out each oath, I wondered what Socrates would make of such a performance: and at this thought I couldn't help laughing out loud.

The Greek swung round and said to me, in excellent French: 'It's no laughing matter, young fellow. You ought to be crying, you really ought. Shall I tell you something? I spent years in the Belgian Congo. That's right, the *Belgian Congo*. They've got proper roads over there – tarred surface, filling-stations, the works. The Belgians have done a good job in the Congo, believe you me. But the French here' – he laughed sardonically – 'they only work the place for what they can get out of it, the greedy so-and-sos.'

Kritikos pulled a sour face, shrugged his shoulders in disgust, and said no more. The other passengers, all Negroes, turned their eyes anxiously in my direction. They looked as though they were afraid I might not continue with this Homeric argument. They came of a race who enjoy nothing better than a good brawl, with fists or words – even when conducted in a language of which they have, at the best, a very slight smattering.

'In that case,' I said tentatively, 'why didn't you stay in the Belgian Congo?'

I did not for a moment think of actually defending French colonialism: even in those days I knew that all colonial systems have one thing in common, a belief in the efficacy of the big stick. But at the same time my question, considered in purely logical terms, did have a certain pertinence. At the

3

sound of my voice all the faces turned back to Kritikos. He sat there, in some puzzlement it seemed, his Mediterranean-blue eyes contemplating my miserable person. Finally he shrugged his shoulders yet again, and turned his back on me. The passengers grinned.

'You don't understand, you're too young,' the Greek muttered, hunched over his steering-wheel.

The passengers, perceiving that their game-cock – me, that is – had won this bout, merely stared at me with expressions that plainly indicated their feelings. They looked like a bunch of patriots who have just declared a holy war.

But our troubles were not over yet. There sat the bus still, right across the road, with its bonnet hanging over the cliff-edge. The result was that long lines of cars and trucks were forming both behind and in front of us – if we could properly be said to have a front and rear any more – and their drivers, with shouts, curses, and much vigorous blowing of horns, were making it quite plain that they wanted us to clear the road.

Finally Kritikos climbed out of his cab into the rain, slamming the door behind him; and (aided by gesticulations, loud oaths, and other such pantomine) managed to convince his colleagues that he was in no way responsible for what had happened. All the drivers gathered into a group beside the road, the rain streaming off their khaki waterproofs. There was only one white man among them. We sat and watched while they argued. Their first decision was to get all passengers out of the bus. We straggled off, dragging our feet through thick mud, and took shelter in the huts of a tiny settlement not far from the road. Then – I have no very clear idea how – they set about shoving that old cow of a bus back into its proper position. At all events, after an hour's delay the ancient vehicle hove slowly into sight again, skidding on the greasy laterite, snorting and groaning, resigned to its fate.

During these awkward manœuvres my clothes were so splashed and bespattered with mud that they looked as though they had been dyed red. I swore to myself that I would never wear white clothes or shoes to travel in again, even when I was going to see my girl-friend, as I hoped to on this occasion. (She was a childhood sweetheart, and lived near our village.) Normally she was the first person I met when I went home; but this time I never saw her at all. However, that too is another story.

Somehow our bus limped its way into Vimili, the main town of my district. When I say 'the main town' I exaggerate a little: there was little in Vimili except a market and a few primitive shops where the countryfolk would occasionally stock up with provisions. Ah yes: I nearly forgot to mention the Government offices, the police H.Q. and the jail – civic benefits which, in this country, are quite enough to raise a place to the dignity of 'main town' status.

I still had eight or ten miles to go before that dreaded interview with my father. But in Vimili we learnt that the road was blocked just outside the town because of repairs, so I abandoned the bus. It had stopped raining – at least, for the time being. On the other hand, though my case was not particularly heavy, I could hardly carry it (either in my hand or on my head) for the ten long miles that still stood between me and my home.

I spent a good half-hour squatting on the veranda of one of the shops, wondering how to solve my transport problem. Then I suddenly spotted Amou, my youngest aunt, wobbling past on her bicycle. She had never learnt how to ride confidently. She was a widow: her husband had died very young, and she had come back to live with the family again. I shot across the road with desperate agility: here was an unexpected reprieve indeed. 'Oi!' I shouted, rudely, forgetting how often I had been told off at College for my bad manners. My reputation had really been very low, one way and another.

'Lordy!' gasped Aunt Amou, 'it's you, is it? You gave me quite a turn.' She took a deep breath and got into her stride. 'Well, your mother's not at home, nor your father, of course. And your brother – well, your brother's been away so long no one bothers about *him* any more. Your father used to get cross about him at first, but in the end, you know how it is —

Anyway, *I'm* around, and it's lucky I am. The number of times I've wondered what on *earth* would happen to everything if they hadn't got me to look after them. Tell me, is it true that you've failed your thingummy-bob, what d'you call it, your exams?'

I nodded silently.

'That's not so good, you know, especially since it's the first time. Oh well, it's a matter for your father, you'll just have to thrash it out between the two of you.'

I winced.

'Cheer up,' Aunt Amou went on, 'he's away at the moment. Heavens, boy, look at you! Red all over. You look as though you'd been rolling in a puddle. You haven't been fighting with anyone, have you?'

'We had to walk for part of the way,' I said. 'The bus couldn't get up one of the hills —'

She clucked in sympathy. I asked her, not really believing it myself, if she had been looking for me.

'Lordy, no. D'you think I get all the latest news from the Almighty? Breakfast-gossip with God, h'm? I had no idea you were coming this morning. All we knew in the village was that you'd been failed.'

She grabbed my bag with her usual brisk liveliness.

'The road,' I ventured, 'seems to be blocked for wheeled traffic —'

'That's right,' said Aunt Amou, 'so you're going to walk all the way on your flat feet, dear. Don't gape at me like a codfish, boy! I've got some shopping to do, but when I'm finished I'll go on ahead with your little case – it'll fit quite nicely on the luggage-grid. Be off with you now: it might come on to rain again.'

I didn't ask her what shopping she had to do, though I felt a little sad, nostalgic even, at being reminded of her husband. I had been about as intimate with him as any child can be with a grown-up. I couldn't ask this woman tactless questions: she was my aunt, after all, a person older than myself. All the same, I couldn't help thinking about her late husband.

I plodded on down the muddy road, thunder growing and

6

muttering overhead. My damp mud-spattered clothes made me clammily aware of my own body; my mind was full of sour splenetic thoughts, mostly picked up from gloomy articles in the weekly Press. Women are all the same, I told myself. There wasn't a penny to choose between my sweetheart and my aunt; the girl simply wasn't worth all my dreams and longings. But there's really no point in mentioning her here; she plays no part in this story.

Except for the stormy explanatory scene which still had to be faced, home life seemed to be beginning in a fairly normal way.

I knew this chap Niam about as well as I did any of my cousins, which means hardly at all. It was a long time since I had spent three months on end in the village. Niam was about thirty-five. I wouldn't have supposed, from what I knew of him, that he took any very great interest in his wife – while she was still around, that is. I would have thought that if she walked out on him Niam would have been more relieved than sorry. But, as Aunt Amou told me, when she actually *did* disappear, Niam's home-life became completely chaotic. He got in a frightful state. What was worse, said Aunt Amou, he was a coward.

'Fancy, the way he treated her, the stupid brute! No better than a dog. She worked hard enough, too. Worse than a dog, really, because a dog – a bitch, anyway – can always have litters, but she never had a child. Niam thought that gave him the right to insult and maltreat her all day long. *Men!* Stupid, pretentious, conceited beasts —'

I am convinced today that Aunt Amou had a personal obsession about all this because she had never managed to conceive herself, and now it looked as though she would never have a child at all – not only because her husband was dead, but through her own sterility.

Later, my mother gave me her version of the trouble between Niam and his wife. According to her, Mrs Niam had had a scandalous liaison with some young fellow from the town, a market-boy by trade, who made her presents of dress-material and other attractive fripperies, ideal for seducing a young woman. It may seem surprising that my mother took such a disapproving attitude to this affair, since in our country what Europeans describe as 'adultery' (a word loaded with heavy puritanism) doesn't on the whole provoke really violent reactions, even if people aren't entirely indifferent to such peccadilloes. Still, you must bear in mind that normally these affairs are restricted to members of the same tribe; they are, so to speak, a family affair. The seriousness with which any adultery is regarded is in exact proportion to the physical or social 'distance' between the two tribes – those, that is, of the cuckolded husband and the intrusive lover respectively. For a woman to grant her favours to a man from a neighbouring tribe is bad enough; if she goes with some rootless stranger she is, in all intents and purposes, deliberately giving the most deadly insult possible to her own kin.

My mother's prejudice against Niam's wife, however, was chiefly due to the fact that, after years of marriage, the woman for some inscrutable reason had still failed to produce a child. It is the usual thing among our people for all childless wives to suffer a curious kind of communal anathema, the origins of which must be sought in the spiritual beliefs of our Bantu ancestors. Once a married woman has had a child, all her caprices and infidelities are excused. But you know all about that.

To come to the point: Niam's wife had decamped. I don't know what minor incident finally provoked the crisis, what last straw broke this female camel's back, or even which of the two was ultimately responsible. The important thing is that one morning, when he got up, Niam perceived to his astonishment that his better half had vanished, taking all her own property with her. That, by the way, is how they always manage it: hence their nickname of fly-by-nights.

A few days later our family heard that Niam's wife had gone back to her father. So far her behaviour had followed the usual pattern. The unexpected thing was that she swore (it was said) never to return to her husband's house again.

Some months passed. At first Niam put a fine face on the business, declaring jauntily that he'd seen this kind of thing before: his wife had indulged in several previous escapades of the sort and had always come back in the end.

'I am the earth she rests on,' he declared fatuously. 'By herself she is nothing but a dead leaf that has broken loose from the tree. For all her flutterings and gyrations, in the end she cannot prevent herself falling to the ground.'

All the same, he was by no means sure that on this occasion the dead leaf would obey the laws of gravity. Already – even in Niam – the hope of seeing the happy event take place like clockwork was fading steadily as day followed day.

After six months of this, Niam grew impatient. First of all he paid a visit one evening to Bikokolo, a venerable old patriarch and the village Solomon. He confessed (not without an effort, since his pride was enormous) that he wanted to get his wife back; he desperately needed her to run the house for him. In fact, he had an even more pressing reason: since his wife's departure he had lost a whole season's groundnut crop through lack of anyone to work in his fields.

Old Bikokolo, who could take a hint as well as the next man, sketched out a line of conduct for him to follow, and, at the end of the interview, strongly advised him to swallow his vanity and pride, at least for a while. After all, he pointed out, the recovery of a flagrantly rebellious wife was a serious matter. Niam reflected, as he went away, that it was easier to give such advice than take it.

After this, guided both by the old man's suggestions and his own peculiar code of behaviour (which forbade him to take any direct part in a bargaining deal, so as not to lose face in front of his wife), he got in touch with his father-in-law through several intermediaries, somehow giving the impression that he had nothing to do with the move at all. The whole village soon found out that Niam had opened negotiations with his inlaws, and had even sent them presents. But this was nothing to the general astonishment felt when Niam's father-in-law (having accepted his gifts) made the following pronouncement.

9

'My daughter,' he declared, 'is quite old enough to know what she wants – and, more to the point, what she *doesn't* want.'

This flat rejection of a lawful demand, made by a mere father-in-law, too, was regarded as completely scandalous.

Everyone in the village began to wonder just what these people were holding out for, what they really wanted.

Gradually, thanks chiefly to Bikokolo's sage counsel, Niam began to realize the unpleasant alternatives with which he was faced. He could either go on sending presents to his in-laws – a situation in which, so to speak, there is no ceiling to the bidding – or else he could enter the lists in person. This would be a terrible humiliation for him, the kind of humiliation which makes it pretty certain that one's wife will no longer give one that respect to which a husband worthy of the name, a Lord and Master in fact, is lawfully entitled.

Niam spent weeks trying to get himself out of this embarrassing fix. During this period he would wander through the fields like a ghost, watching other men's wives at work. There they all were, bent double, and scratching away obediently with their little hoes. It looked as though he was going to lose another groundnut crop.

Some of the women would stand up as he passed, and call out to him: 'Hullo there, Niam! Cleared your field yet?'

Niam would say yes, he had, but what good would that do him?

'A big one?' they would ask.

'Sure: enormous.'

'Did it burn well?'

'Wonderfully.'

'But you can't let the whole crop rot now: what a wicked waste!'

At this point Niam would ask if they expected him to go and hoe the field himself.

'Plenty of men do, Niam,' they would say.

'Not me.'

'Pride'll be the death of you, Niam,' they would say, and

then, relenting: 'Ah, go on with you. Come and have supper at our place tonight.'

In the end, for all his efforts, Niam failed to find any solution to his dilemma. It was at this stage of the affair that I made my appearance. Niam decided that I had been sent providentially to help him, and at once thought up a perfectly diabolical plan. He was like some desperate general throwing his last reserves into the breach.

He came and called on us the day after my arrival, the first morning of my vacation. What with the thought of another exam hanging over me, I was already a bit lacking in holiday spirit. He outlined his scheme in an off-hand, cynical sort of way. I was to go to his in-laws' place and take a strong line with them. If necessary I could bang my fist on the table for emphasis. They would be scared and hand over his wife, and I would bring her back. It sounded a shady sort of proposition; but to be quite honest, the thought uppermost in my mind was that it meant going on a longish journey. Now the one thing I wanted to do at that precise moment was to sleep off my little set-back. Not the sleep of the just, perhaps, but the sleep of a failed exam-candidate, which is almost as well-deserved. So I refused, and Aunt Amou backed me up.

'*Really*, Niam,' she said, in her most cutting voice, 'what frightful manners you have! Can't you leave people in peace for a *moment*?'

But Niam had thought everything out beforehand. He knew perfectly well I would refuse, and had taken the precaution of getting Bikokolo's support in the matter. The old man had virtually powers of life and death over everyone in our village.

'A pity your father isn't here, my dear cousin,' Niam said. 'But Bikokolo *is* here, and agrees with me. Do you understand? It isn't just my personal affair any longer. It's a tribal matter. My wife doesn't belong to me exclusively, if you follow me; she's tribal property. So the present situation affects all of us. If your father was here, he would be the first to make you go and interview these people.'

I asked for two days to think the proposal over, and Niam

gave me twenty-four hours. I then threatened, quite bluntly, to call the whole thing off and not to listen to another word. Niam walked out, stood in the village square, and began to declaim in a loud voice all the reasons why I was under an obligation to perform a mission of such public importance. Obviously he was getting all my aunts and uncles as witnesses of my refusal.

The whole thing was beginning to bore me. Aunt Amou grumbled and cursed, but with less and less vigour as she sized up the situation. It was plain enough that we'd been caught, fair and square, by a proper conspiracy. Niam had organized the whole thing with masterly finesse: he had every male inhabitant of the village in his pocket. I still don't know how he managed it. They all expressed their desire for me to go and put the wind up Niam's in-laws. But since my failure in the exam I no longer had any confidence in myself.

Niam now revealed himself as a proper village Demosthenes, especially since it was his own cause he was pleading. There he stood in the market square like some shyster advocate, talking his head off. It was a classic performance. Rhetorical flourishes, careful repetition and emphasis, sly insinuations; hostile arguments set up and demolished, apparent surrender followed by immediate counter-attack, he tried them all. He roared with laughter, and produced nicely calculated exclamations of surprise. He asked his supporters questions and got exactly the answers he wanted. People came out on to their doorsteps to listen to him.

Eventually Aunt Amou couldn't stand this comedy any longer. She marched up to Niam and set about him.

'Aren't you ashamed to drag this poor boy into your dirty lies? He's just a child – you were a grown man when he was born. You'd hear all about it if his father was here, you filthy beast!'

This violent and unexpected attack rather took Niam's breath away. But the next moment, pat on his cue, Bikokolo himself came to the unfortunate Niam's rescue. It was like a scene from a rather bad film. I had thought at first that it was rather unwise of Niam to follow the old man's advice. Now here he came in person, waddling along with slow patriarchal dignity, rolling his enormous naked paunch, and smacking away at his legs and back with a fly-whisk. First of all he addressed Aunt Amou.

'My child,' he said, 'what are you worried about? The boy's father is absent, agreed. But he is not in the least anxious about his son. He can attend to his business with an easy mind. He knows that in me the boy has a father who cares for him even more closely than he does himself. Dear me, if the good man were to have heard those – those blasphemous remarks of yours just now, I don't know what he might have done. Little Medza here is very young, to be sure. No one would deny it. Almost a child, as you said; we all remember the day he was born. But anyone would think we were asking him to go and put Niam's wife in the family way to hear you carry on —'

A burst of ribald laughter interrupted him.

'Well, why not?' shouted one of my cousins, about my own age. He sounded a bit peeved. 'He's capable of it, isn't he?'

The laughter became almost hysterical; even Bikokolo joined in.

'I'm not casting doubts on our young friend's virility,' he said at length. 'But that's not what he's being asked to do. He only has to make the trip there and put the fear of God into those savages. It's not much really —'

While the old man had been talking I had been thinking hard. Suddenly I discovered, in the arsenals of my Cartesian dialectic, an argument which seemed absolutely unanswerable, and which, I thought, would win me a victory over even so ferocious an opposition as this. It would be like the exploding cartridge that knocks out a wild beast in the very act of charging the hunter – except that in the present case I wasn't, so to speak, the hunter. I walked out and joined the meeting with the firm intention of keeping back my bombshell till I'd exhausted every other tub-thumping trick I knew – feigned hesitation, suspense, irony, the whole gamut of theatrical rhetoric.

'Listen carefully, gentlemen,' I said. 'I have just been sitting an examination. Have any of you the least idea what preparing for an examination and sitting it entails? No, of course you haven't. Gentlemen, try and imagine something worse, far worse, than working in a plantation with a machete from dawn till dusk —'

I paused for a moment before going on, pleased with the powerful impression this comparison had produced on my audience.

'After this exhausting labour, I have come back among you for a rest. But the first thing you do is demand that I should go off on another journey, undertake a special mission on your behalf. Please note that I'm not refusing your request. You've made it quite clear, and I accept the fact, that this woman was our common possession – though one would hardly have guessed it while she was among us – and that the affair is therefore the common concern of our tribe. But there's one thing I still don't quite understand. Why me rather than anyone else? Why should I be able to put the wind up these people? Older men have made representations to them, and they haven't batted an eyelid. What power have *I* got that no one else has?'

The effect of my remarks was considerable. A murmur of disappointment was audible from every veranda: I almost felt sorry for them. Then one of my uncles, a far-sighted man, said: 'I'm not absolutely sure that the boy's a congenital simpleton – though it wouldn't surprise me in the least – but he obviously has no idea what he's being asked to do now. What's the point of being surprised and vexed at that? Why not explain the situation to him a bit more clearly? You can't expect him to understand it just like that, can you? Use your common sense. He's away at school most of the time. He only comes home occasionally. The really surprising thing is that he's still familiar with our tribal wisdom and customs at all. Stop gaping, and *explain*.'

That was, more or less, the gist of his speech.

The old patriarch turned slowly towards me. I was somewhat crestfallen at the way my rhetorical gambit had misfired. A supremely complacent and patronizing smile hovered round Bikololo's mouth; it was the kind of smile I associated with that assumed by a fourth-form Latin master when one of his pupils produces a really barbarous howler.

'My boy,' Bikokolo said, 'don't you *really* understand?' He then proceeded to tell me a longish story based on one of our national myths. He garnished his narrative with endless digressions, dialogue that ran to monologue, and the kind of declamation that got him a great name at tribal palavers. He had a curious trick of confusing fact with legend, and treating the wisdom drawn from personal experience on exactly the same terms as those gnomic saws he inherited from our most ancient traditions. Here is his story, reduced to its basic essentials.

There was once a man who, all unbeknown to himself, spoke with the voice of the thunder. Imagine his astonishment when, one day, he was sent on a very similar mission to that which faced me now. In particular he asked himself what supernatural power *he* commanded to make him succeed where others had failed.

'My son,' the old man concluded, 'when this story is recited after my death, you will be its hero. *You* are that formidable man; *you* speak with the voice of the thunder, and have never suspected your own powers. Shall I tell you what your special thunder is? Your certificates, your learning, your knowledge of white men's secrets. Have you any idea what these up-country bushmen will quite seriously believe about you? That you only have to write a letter in French, or speak French to the nearest District Officer, to have anyone you like imprisoned, or get any personal favour you want. That's the kind of idiocy you'll find waiting for you.'

Aunt Amou and I were struck dumb by this. We saw we were really done for when Bikokolo, having apparently decided that my agreement was now an understood thing about which there was no more to be said, passed to practical tips about my mission.

'When you reach Kala,' he told me – 'that's the village where Niam's wife was born – you will ask for the house of a man called Mama. He's by way of being your uncle, your father's cousin, anyway. You may not know him, but he knows all about you. You're going to stay with him during your visit. My boy, his hospitality is absolutely unrivalled: just wait and see what a spread he lays on for you. You won't be sorry you went, I can tell you that. You'll be treated like royalty.' The old man giggled to himself. 'You will also meet Mama's son Zambo, your cousin. He's a big fellow, just like his father, looks more like his brother than his son.'

My interest had quickened somewhat after listening to the old man's recital. To be sure, I wondered whether his views on the Kala bushmen were not a little exaggerated. But – perhaps precisely because this query suggested itself to me – something was slowly stirring inside me, a siren voice which I recognized as the love of adventure. An *easy* adventure, among comparatively simple people, is the secret wish and aim of every adventurer. When you come to think of it, the very existence of adventurers is only made possible by the survival of primitive, simple-minded tribes. When the latter finally vanish, they will take the former with them; they are like Siamese twins, who can't survive independently. My imagination was running away with me. The ploughed student was transformed into a brigand chief, a pirate, a true Conquistador. My fancy settled firmly for the Conquistadors. The thought of being adopted into this exclusive clan elated me: my promotion had indeed been rapid.

I told myself I wasn't really as tired as all that, fundamentally. Lightheartedly I agreed to undertake the mission.

In a fever of enthusiasm I armed myself for the fray – or, to be more exact, sorted out my best clothes. I emptied my bag of everything that would make it unnecessarily heavy – books in particular. Aunt Amou couldn't get over it.

One problem presented itself: how was I to get there? I asked for this to be settled on the spot, as I intended starting early next morning.

'No trouble about *that*, my dear cousin,' said Niam breezily; 'you'll go by bus, of course.'

'Getting a bit airy-fairy, aren't you?' I asked. My voice was already taking on that virile self-assurance that can be produced only by the knowledge that one is absolutely indispensable. '*You'll go by bus*. So I go by bus. What happens then? Can you see me walking ten or twelve miles lugging this case? I suppose you'd like me to carry it on my head. Why not on the little finger of my left hand while you're about it?'

Bikokolo laughed quietly. 'The boy has a point there,' he said. 'Let's see, now. Fifteen miles by road and then about twelve more along a forest track, that's right, isn't it?'

'That's right,' several voices replied in an off-hand way, as if to say the place was just round the corner.

'Can the bus or any kind of car travel on this track?' Bikokolo asked, with the air of a man who knows in advance exactly what answer he will get.

'Not a hope,' said some wag or other, 'not a hope of getting a car down *this* track.'

'That's what I thought,' said the old man. 'If these up-country bushmen round Kala saw cars every day, I can't see any reason why they shouldn't be as smart as we are. Come on, give the boy some transport. He deserves it.'

Encouraged by this support, I announced that what I needed was a bicycle, and that nothing else would do.

In fact I was dreaming of a richly caparisoned horse.

'First-rate notion!' Niam exclaimed. 'Your Aunt Amou's bicycle, just the thing!'

'What's got into you, you impertinent creature?' demanded my aunt, in her sourest, most contemptuous voice. '*My* bicycle? What's wrong with yours? Any man your age has got his own bicycle. Why haven't you? Wouldn't the shopkeepers touch your money? *My bicycle*, indeed! Are you willing to give me another one to ride into town tomorrow, eh? *And* every day afterwards? Where can *you* find me another bicycle?'

This delighted me. I had no intention of turning up in Kala on Aunt Amou's bicycle. It was a woman's model, far too low in the saddle for me, and would have looked out of place anyway with a man riding it.

Niam said, with heavy sarcasm: 'And while we're on the subject, *you* might tell us what you find to do all day in town.' He wanted to needle Aunt Amou. They hated each other, and not only on account of this job Niam had landed me with. A long history of squabbles and grudges divided them, but owing to my long absences and total absorption in my studies, I had very little knowledge of just what they were. Anyway, that's another story too.

It took another long discussion to establish officially what we had all known for years: the obvious fact that the only man's bicycle in the area belonged to the local Chief, who lived not far away. The next move was plain enough: we had to get the Chief to agree to lend me his machine.

This local Chief of ours was an ancient lecher with remarkable staying powers. Despite his age, he had got hold of the six prettiest girls in the district and was always on the lookout for more. Like most Chiefs, he occupied an influential position in the community, with all the usual perquisites. He was a rich man by our standards and lived in an imposing villa; his general way of life was luxurious in the extreme. The Colonial Administration (who had nominated him in the first place) buttered him up. In return, he obeyed their commands like a robot and knew they would never throw him out. In the days of the forced labour gangs he had been feared by everyone because he betrayed fugitives to the authorities and acted as an informer. He used our traditional tribal hierarchy as a vehicle for his underhand intrigues, and flouted our laws and customs when he no longer needed them.

There wouldn't have been any trouble from him if he hadn't been keeping a suspicious eye on me already. (*Me*, the star in the ascendant, the coming man of the tribe!) But the reason why this local politician, this village dictator, did me the honour of numbering me among his Opposition was rather unexpected. It was not (as might have been thought) because of my subversive ideas, or my wide circle of acquaintances among

18

'foreigners' and possible enemies outside the tribe, or anything that could have justified the least scrap of public, official suspicion. No; it was simply because I made eyes at his wives. He said so, and he almost certainly believed it. I did, in fact, do something of the sort, but not exactly when he thought I did. Anyway, the girls themselves (who were, undeniably, attractive in the extreme) tempted me in the most shameless way. Despite my reserved nature, I wouldn't have answered for what I might have got up to if it hadn't been for my mother, who didn't like that sort of thing.

Well, there was a long discussion, to which I, for obvious reasons, wasn't invited. Nobody told me what went on at it, but the upshot was that our Chief deigned to add his little brick to the national edifice – the recovery of Niam's wife, that is. He lent me his bicycle, but on one condition: the whole tribe would be held responsible for my behaviour to his harem during the rest of the vacation. The treaty was concluded without further difficulty.

The bastard! I never had had any great love for him, but I cheerfully hoped he would drop dead that day. My hatred could hardly go deeper; as time went on it simply spread out, till today it embraces not only the polygamous as a class, but also every kind of monopolist, profiteer, extortionate employer, and bloated fat-belly.

Early the next morning I mounted my splendid machine (described by the manufacturers as 'an aristocrat among bicycles') and pedalled off with all the vigour proper to a Conquistador, even if only a would-be one. With its big wheels and well-oiled pedals it went along at a tremendous lick. In midflight I slowed down a bit, fascinated by the spectacle of the road unwinding beneath me in an endless red ribbon, like some benevolent fairy's conjuring trick. The chain whirred round like a rosary; it made me think 'of Pizarro's steel-shod horse, thundering along the tracks that crossed the vast kingdom of the Incas. The rhythmic, metallic sound hypnotized me.

Occasionally I stopped, and with one foot just touching the

ground while the other remained, as it were, in the stirrup, I gazed at the vast panorama lying open to my future exploits. (This 'vast panorama' was for the most part restricted to a seedy vista of tree-trunks lining the road, oppressive in the most literal sense.) Then there was this strange name of mine, Medza. If I added one tiny syllable, only one, it would be transformed into a real Conquistador's name. Medzaro! – just like Pizarro, or near enough, anyway.

Then I turned off the road on to the track through the forest. It wasn't a bad track at all: I hardly had to slacken speed on it. However, on several occasions I was obliged to cross an unbridged river, and then I would dismount and wade across with the bicycle slung round my neck. If Pizarro at times was forced to act as his own groom, that too was, I had no doubt, one of the professional hazards to which he was exposed.

CHAPTER TWO

In which the reader, if he is patient, will make the acquaintance of Kala's inhabitants, and learn something of their customs and aspirations – the latter being essentially peaceful, even if somewhat new-fangled, a demonstration of the fact that war is not necessary to progress.

The reader will also learn of our hero's adventures among the natives of this strange country – adventures which might more properly be described as sentimental rather than picaresque.

I REACHED Kala about three o'clock in the afternoon. My entry was anything but triumphal – the journey through that hot, dank forest had considerably dampened my enthusiasm and panache – and passed, in fact, almost unnoticed. There was an excellent reason for this; and, indeed, I was at once enlightened as to how far the term 'savage', used that morning by old Bikokolo, was applicable to the local inhabitants.

Just outside the village a remarkable spectacle presented itself to my astonished gaze. It was not the setting which struck me so much as the primitive savagery which animated every participant in the business. There was a sports ground here, a very good one for a mere wattle-and-mud village, and dotted round it were one or two biggish huts, their verandas crowded with spectators anxious to get out of the sun. On the sports ground were about twenty big toughs, bare-legged and bare-chested, engaged in a game whose warlike nature even

21

the Spartans would have recognized. I jumped off my bicycle and wheeled it as close as I could without anyone, performer or spectator, even noticing my presence.

It was baking hot.

Each team consisted of ten or twelve young men lined up in single file, Indian fashion. Thus only the two leaders of each side were actually facing each other, at two or three yards' distance: their supporters backed them up from behind. Each man carried a long, whippy, heavy assegai, its point carefully sharpened. They brandished these weapons in a most dangerous fashion. Right at the end of each file, as far as possible from the captain, that is, stood the strongest man in the team. This man would pick up a ball about the size of a football, made of some hard, heavy, yet porous wood, spin round two or three times like a weight-putter, and throw the ball as hard as he could along the ground. It sped away at a tremendous speed, bumping and bouncing over the rough ground; and as it went the long pointed assegais whizzed out at it so hard and quickly that it was a miracle that no one was hit each time. Often the ball was stopped in mid-flight, pierced clean through by a particularly accurate shot. Then the team's supporters would cheer like mad, and all the lucky marksman's companions smother him with kisses. Then the referee, squatting in one corner of the field, would score five long lines on the ground to the credit of the lucky team. At the end of a match these lines were totted up. When they changed service, so to speak, all the players turned in the same direction – facing the hefty fellow who was going to throw the ball into play, five throws at a time.

I was astonished by the whole thing, though in the end I remembered that when we were about six or so we used to play a similar sort of game at home. But in our case it was a childish pastime, a mere survival from former times, and not taken in the least seriously. At Kala, to judge by this match, it was still going very strong indeed.

From the cheers and shouts of encouragement I gathered that the village of Kala was challenging another village for top place in the league, and that the match I was watching would decide the issue.

Having first taken a bird's-eye, panoramic view of the scene, I now began to examine it in detail. The first thing that caught my eye was a great hulking devil in the Kala team, who had such enormous muscles that I concluded he must have bought them on the instalment system. There was simply no other explanation possible. He was tall and flat-footed, with a disproportionately lengthy torso which, nevertheless, he carried very badly. His buttocks were incredibly slender, yet he retained the country native's slight pot-belly, due to a habitually rough and meagre diet. He was like a kind of human baobab tree.* Naturally, he was the one who threw the ball for his team. I had no difficulty in finding out that his name was Zambo: every time he threw the ball the spectators shouted his name in chorus, as though he had been a friendly God to be supplicated at the siege of Troy.

'Zambo, son of Mama!' they yelled, 'Zambo, son of Mama! Zambo! Zambo!'

I found it hard to convince myself that this monster was really my cousin, the young man from whom old Bikokolo had promised me so wonderful a reception. By what miraculous process, I asked myself, could this man be related to me in any way?

When Zambo (son of Mama) wound himself up to 'serve', he shot the ball into play with such force – presumably so as not to favour those of his own team who stood closest to him – that there was very seldom a chance to hit it at all. Generally when an assegai struck the ground, the ball Zambo had thrown had passed by a couple of seconds earlier. Besides, very few of the players in either team made any very serious attempt to hit the ball when this great ape was in charge of it; they were more concerned with getting out of its way. Since they could hardly see it flash by, they preferred to keep clear of it: for them it was a thunderbolt, a divine force both invisible and

* A tree native to West Africa, the trunk of which is anything up to 30 feet in girth. Also known as the Monkey-Bread. – TRS.

blind. When Zambo picked up the ball, in fact, it was transformed.

On the other hand, however hard his opposite number 'served', Zambo never flinched from the murderous projectile's path. He watched it hawk-like, dodging round it with fancy footwork, and his shot almost always went home. Then he would clasp his hands above his head like a boxer and himself yell: 'Zambo, son of Mama!' as if to proclaim his victory.

I still remember one extraordinary incident which brought most of the spectators to their feet with exclamations of horror. The ball, pitched on this occasion by the opposition, was whizzing towards the Kala team at a really colossal speed. They all gave it a pretty wide berth, as though it were a charging rhino – all, that is, except Zambo, who stood his ground, bounding about like a huge antelope and squaring up to his target with truly heroic sang-froid. But in the split second befor the ball reached him, it hit either a stone or some ridge in the ground, and shot up into the air. It rose so sharply that it would have knocked Zambo's head off (he was a very tall man) if he hadn't ducked like a flash. Even in this crisis he still found time to fling his assegai into the air. I don't know exactly what happened; I shut my eyes at the crucial moment and, anyway, it was all over in an instant. But when I dared look again, the sports ground was echoing with the frantic cheers of all the spectators. The ball lay at Zambo's feet, pierced clean through; and Zambo himself was glaring at it, as though hypnotizing it into yet humbler submission.

The whole match was a kind of Zambo benefit; it was not the Kala team that won, but Zambo on his own. I was proud of my cousin, but nevertheless felt an instinctive fear and repugnance at the very sight of him – perhaps because the weak are naturally terrified by strength, and therefore come to hate it. The temporary Conquistador in me suddenly decided that it was far preferable to be a ploughed student again. All I wanted to do at that moment was get back into my ordinary clothes and put my best suit away in the wardrobe again.

The sun was sinking behind the forest ridge like a scuttled and blown-up ship, and at last the match came to an end. The twenty young men were completely exhausted, especially after having played tag for so long with that lethal ball, in a kind of endless dance. Zambo left the field escorted by a crowd of boys singing patriotic hymns (or something of the sort) and several girls, who kept up an ear-splitting series of triumphal war-whoops. Like a young god he marched proudly past me. and I stood there, petrified.

Yet after he had moved on, for some inexplicable reason he turned and looked back: our eyes met. His gaze lingered on me, and he knitted his brows thoughtfully. Then he turned away and moved off with his escort again, but almost at once turned back for the second time. After a moment's hesitation he came over to me. It was only then that his attendants became aware of my presence, and took in the fact that I was dressed like a townsman and was wheeling a magnificent bicycle.

My athletic cousin was the first to break the silence, in some evident confusion. He could hardly have been more confused than I was.

'I cannot help thinking I know you,' he said.

'It would not surprise me to hear it.' I tried to make my voice sound dignified. Dignity was the one advantage I had left.

'But it is probable that you, on the other hand, do not know me,' Zambo went on. 'The circumstances in which we have met before have always been unfavourable to your making my real acquaintance.'

'Really?' I said. 'Where would that have been?'

'It's too long a story. Townsfolk like you hardly ever bother to get to know your relations. With us it's different.'

I said: 'You are Mama's son, though aren't you? David Mama, that is?'

'Yes, indeed. Your cousin, and at your service.'

'At my service?'

'Little cousin,' Zambo said, 'you can't imagine how

delighted and honoured I am to be able to talk to you today. You can have no idea —'

Delighted and honoured? To talk to *me*? I couldn't understand it. I must have misheard him. My athletic cousin did not, however, sound as though he were joking. For a moment I really believed I was going to faint with shock. There stood Zambo, smiling benignly at me and exposing all his magnificent teeth : benevolent, friendly, fraternal, even a little obsequious. His whole attitude was exactly what was needed to reassure me completely; yet somehow reassurance failed to come. Try to imagine a poor insignificant creature, an ex-Conquistador retreating (after a brief career) in some confusion, a mere failed student once more, who is confronted with the spectacle of a young god falling down at his feet and worshipping him. For a moment I hated my cousin. I resented this unexpected reversal of our roles, and the way in which, for the third time that day, I had been forced to revise my estimate of my own strength.

Besides, Zambo was not alone in his disconcerting attitude. All the young boys and girls who had been singing *his* praises now turned and clustered round *me*, displaying the indiscriminate admiration and generally unrestrained behaviour which (I supposed) were only to be found among such up-country bushmen.

'Look at his clothes,' one said. 'He's a proper town boy, isn't he?'

'Oh, he's a town boy all right. Look at that bike. What a swell he must be!'

'Good-looking, don't you think?'

'*And* young.'

I felt most embarrassed. I wanted to tell them that I wasn't a swell at all, and nearly as old as my cousin Zambo, their champion. But this first experience of such imbecile admiration paralysed me. I had been brought up for six years or more to believe in modesty, even on occasion humility, and I was beginning to resent their attentions. Zambo (who continued to grin obsequiously at me) must in the end have noticed my embarrassment, for he invited me home to get a little rest, as he put it. I accepted thankfully. He insisted on pushing the bicycle.

While we walked, with our common fans stretched out behind us like a pack of hounds that has picked up an unexpected scent, Zambo asked me why I had come to Kala. I gave him a brief account of the affair, and told him – with careful emphasis – that I was to stay with his father, if this was not inconvenient. When I mentioned this caveat, Zambo looked as astonished as if his grandmother (who had died ten years earlier) had suddenly materialized in front of him and asked, very humbly, for a drink.

'But, little cousin,' he protested, 'we should be highly honoured to have you in our house, naturally – the pleasure is all ours —'

Honoured again. What did it all mean? At this point he launched into a long rambling speech of which I remember only the essential point, which was that everyone ought to show me great respect because of my learning and diplomas. I reflected that my family back home had seen the matter in a rather different light.

My relatives in Kala lived very near the centre of the village. When we reached their hut, Zambo sent the fans packing without ceremony. (Some of them looked as though they intended to come in with us.)

'Go on, off with you,' he said. 'Don't you realize that the stranger is our guest? He must be allowed to rest for a little.'

They hung their heads and slunk off.

My uncle Mama and his wife were still in the fields.

The 'hut' was a fairly imposing building, both on account of its size and the quantity of furniture and fittings it contained. David Mama was a cabinet-maker by trade, but this did not stop him working in the fields on occasion.

The furniture was clumsily made and of poor finish, being constructed with an extremely hard type of wood. The odd thing was that when, a little later, Zambo took me to inspect his father's workshop, I could quite honestly admire the elegance, light finish, and perfection of line which characterized the pieces on the bench. Uncle Mama was a queer kind of craftsman; he had no notion whatsoever of publicity. He kept the worst jobs for his own use, and let all his best work go elsewhere.

The most remarkable of the many rooms in this so-called 'hut' was a kind of large formal 'dining-room, the walls of which were covered with family photographs instead of the more usual hangings. The whole family were exactly like Zambo: large, tough, and ungainly, to judge from these pictures. Ungainly they were without a doubt – father, mother, and all three children. (The two younger boys were absent during my visit to Kala; from what I heard they sounded near-delinquents.) I stood in front of these photographs, speculating on just what kind of relationship bound me to this endlessly proliferating family, and how much common blood we really had.

I had long ago given up trying to sort out the tangled thread of relationships that might lead me to these people. When I was told 'So-and-so is your cousin' or 'So-and-so is your uncle' I simply accepted the fact without trying to see how it came about. Besides, hitherto consanguinity had brought me only advantages; later I was to learn the rapacity of which relations are capable (a rapacity sanctioned by tradition and custom), and which would inflict serious inroads on my finances. But that too is another story.

My cousin Zambo was generosity itself. When I had told him the details of my mission, an ironic expression which I did not at the time understand flickered over his face for a moment; but he promised me his unconditional assistance in accomplishing what I had to do. This meant that I had an ally in Kala itself – and right on my own doorstep, as it were. Nothing could have helped me more. I had supposed that since my Kala relatives belonged to the same tribe as Niam's wife, they would be obliged, whatever the circumstances, to take her side in the usual way. This would have meant my fighting single-handed against the lot of them – rather as if Menelaus had conceived the rash notion of going off to the Troad to rescue Helen on his own. But Menelaus was a far-sighted man, and preferred to go well escorted, to say the least of it.

A young, extremely presentable girl served us with a light supper: my cousin did not bother to introduce her. So when she had gone back to the kitchen, I asked Zambo if she was his sister or some relative? He burst out laughing, then told me, with shrugging indifference, that she was his mistress.

'Your *mistress*? You mean —'

'Yes, she lives here. Does that surprise you?'

'What about your father?' I inquired, a little breathlessly.

'My father? How do you mean?'

'Doesn't he – mind?'

'Why on earth should he? Because I've got a girl-friend living with me? Really —' and he roared with laughter again.

'Seriously, isn't he annoyed?'

'Of course not, little cousin. He's delighted. She helps Mama in the fields.'

I reflected, gloomily, that if I imported a mistress at home my father would be anything but delighted. Indeed, I had been somewhat taken aback by this revelation, which spoilt my air of sophistication. Zambo was fairly dull-witted, as I later discovered; yet even so he gave me a long look now, half-curious, half-pitying.

'She – she's not your wife, I suppose?' I stammered.

'Oh no! I'm far too young to marry,' Zambo said, teasingly.

'Doesn't your father *really* mind?'

'Why do you suppose he should? Heavens, I'm a grown man, aren't I?'

I could hardly believe my ears. It certainly seemed to be an odd place I had come to. I swallowed several times, and said no more.

Zambo's parents had still not returned from the fields, and night was coming on. Afterwards I found out that in this district people stay out in the fields till it is pitch dark – some of the women, at any rate.

'Little cousin,' Zambo said, 'would you rather wait here and rest till the old folk come back, or come out with me?'

Without quite knowing what impelled me, I said I would like to go out. Zambo took me for a walk through Kala as dusk was falling. It was a huge village, nearly two miles long, its houses ranged along either side of a wide street. This street was rather deceptive; it led to no through road at all. All that happened was that between the edge of the forest and the village the track by which I had travelled broadened out considerably. Kala gave me a simultaneous impression of savagery and security: it was as though one was on a small island, pounded by heavy seas, and yet safe from drowning. The neat huts and bungalows were well spaced out down their long avenue; yet the whole place was encircled and overshadowed by the immensity of the forest, like a gully at the foot of a high cliff. As darkness fell, the street became as busy and animated as any town's native quarter.

Finally Zambo took me into a house where (to judge by the noise) a very drunken party was going on. As we entered we received a roaring welcome that would have done justice to Caesar on his return home from the Gallic Wars. They were celebrating Kala's win in the ball-game that afternoon. I gradually made out all Zambo's team-mates in the seats of honour. Chairs were brought for us, and we were offered palm-wine. A man was playing a guitar, non-stop, with tremendous panache; yet no one except the young girls attending the party seemed to take any pleasure in his music. He also sang ballads which sounded like love-songs, transposing the same words and verses from one tune to another without making any attempt at variety or improvisation. He was a very proficient guitarist, but unimaginative in the extreme.

'Listen to me, everybody!' Zambo shouted, clapping his hands.

'Who dares to call for silence here?' someone asked.

'Zambo, son of Mama!' several voices answered.

'Himself in person!' thundered my cousin.

In a second you could have heard a pin drop.

'Dear brothers,' Zambo began, 'young lords of Kala —'

'Long live Kala, the winning village! Long live Kala, the

30

winning village!' they all shouted, with such well-drilled spontaneity that the demonstration sounded as though it had been rehearsed days before.

'Listen to me carefully, dear brothers,' Zambo went on. 'Listen, and know what good fortune has befallen me. This young man you see sitting beside me is none other than my cousin from the town, that same prodigy of whom I have so often spoken to you. When I boasted of him you thought I was pulling your legs, do you remember? Well, here he is : take a good look at him. He was born on the road, and his name is Medza – don't worry if you find it odd, it's common where he comes from.

'So let me present to you my dear cousin. Medza. You could search the whole district round for two hundred, three, four, five hundred miles, and I wager you wouldn't find a man, white or black, as learned and knowledgeable as he is —'

I tried to protest, but Zambo was well away by now.

'When I used to tell you that the blood which runs in my veins is noble,' he shouted, 'that I have an aristocratic ancestry —'

'Zambo!' they roared in chorus, 'Zambo, son of Mama!'

'*Lui-même en chair et en os!*'* replied my cousin, suddenly breaking into French. Then he went on in our own tongue once more : 'Take a good look at this boy. He is my favourite cousin. He has been at school since he was a child, and never gone anywhere else. He's won every diploma you clodhoppers can think of, and a good few more besides. Today he sits on the same benches as the sons of white men. But – mark my words – even the white professors themselves are scratching their heads over what sort of diploma they can give him next. He has learnt all they can teach him. Yet he's still a young boy : look at him. Well, fellows, what do you think of him?'

'He's certainly a person to be reckoned with,' replied someone in conciliatory tones. 'Yes, that he certainly is.'

'I don't need to tell you to treat him with all the respect due to him,' Zambo insisted.

* 'Himself in the flesh!'

31

'Anyone would do that without being told,' a voice called out. The sweat was fairly running off me by now.

'Well, that's all I have to tell you,' Zambo concluded. He was beaming with delight, and still obviously excited. It would have put me much more at ease if I could have believed he had played this brisk little comedy with his tongue well in his cheek. Now I was forced to realize that my cousin had meant every word he said – that the whole thing was quite serious. What a mistake!

The party was well under way again. All the young folk came up to me one by one and shook my hand with great friendliness and respect. I might have been a king, and they my vassals lining up to swear the Oath of Allegiance.

Everyone there was young, and the atmosphere was more sympathetic, exhilarating even, than anything I had previously experienced. Try to picture a party consisting entirely of young country peasants, completely free and easy in their behaviour, and totally indifferent to strict manners or etiquette – besides being mildly pickled.

Then, suddenly, at a word from someone I couldn't make out, they all began to dance the *assiko*. This dance, as you will know, is still practised only by the up-country bushmen, who think it is the last word in up-to-date fashion. It is a round dance, done to the guitar, with much rocking of shoulders and undulation of buttocks. A master of ceremonies stands in the middle and calls the steps, with much grotesque pantomime, in a queer gibberish supposed to be English.

The men of Kala executed this dance in a manner peculiar to themselves, which I have seen nowhere else. Their enthusiastic abandon was so marked, they indulged in so many flagrantly obscene gestures and so much comic horseplay that it looked as though they were parodying someone or something. But satire implies conscious sophistication, and these dancers simply followed their natural impulses. There could be no possible doubt of that. I became more bewildered every moment.

A young man, slightly more ragged in his attire than the

32

rest, came and sat down beside me on a stool. I was told later that he was commonly known as Duckfoot Johnny, because his feet were not only flat but turned out when he walked. He gave off a powerful stink of palm-wine, probably because he burped titanically every few moments.

'Tell you something,' he breathed confidentially at me. 'Something – *sincere. Sincerely.* All the sincerity in – world. Where was I? Ah yes. This sincere opinion of mine. What I wanna say *is*, 'sfar's *I'm* concerned, you have my un, un-*quali-*fied a'miration. What I think is, compared to me, you're like Godalmighty, 'syou mi' say. My o'l man was ri', y'know. My ol' man used t'say, "My boy, school's not meant for chaps like you. Come an' help me lay traps in foresht, so'sh we can have some deshent *meat. . . ."* J'you know how long I m-managed – get school for?' He giggled maniacally. '*Two yearsh*, Hee-hee-hee! Only two yearsh. You'll shay that isn't much, well, that'sh what I thought, h'm? All shame, I didn' do too badly, only two yearsh. Learnt to write my name, f'rinstance —' He began to scratch on the floor with a twig. 'Firsht, a big B, kind of roundish, see? – Because, y'know, my name'sh Bidzo. Albert Bidzo. Kidsh call me Duckfoot Johnny, but that'sh jusht for a joke. *I* don't care. When kidsh wanna 'muse them-shelvesh, besht let 'em do it. But my real name'sh Albert Bidzo. Only trouble ish, I don't really know how to write "Albert" properly. . . .' He giggled again. 'Can't even *shpell* it. One chap said, ended with a t. Other chap said d. Dunno which to believe. Now, you've got book-learning, could you put my mind at resht on thish p-problem?'

'Certainly. It ends with a t, quite definitely.'

'Ah. A t. That'sh what I thought. Hee-hee-hee!'

Duckfoot Johnny suddenly noticed that my glass was empty. 'Son-of-God!' he bellowed. 'Son-of-God, come here this minute!'

A curious, loose-limbed creature got up at the far end of the hut. He wore a striped, sleeveless shirt and very well-cut khaki shorts, and looked the perfect village gigolo. His eyes glittered with crystalline malice, like vintage wine in a goblet;

a sort of fly-by-night bedroom smile hovered round his lips. Son-of-God, evidently. I learnt afterwards that his father was a part-time Sunday-school teacher, and concluded that this must have given rise to his odd nickname. But I was wrong. In fact, this tag was stuck on the young man because his conduct was so scandalous; it was thought that by thus getting him, so to speak, adopted by God he might yet be saved from hell-fire, since all fathers show infinite indulgence towards their adopted children. But I fancy it started as a witty joke.

'Son-of-God! Petrus!' shouted Duckfoot Johnny.

'Here I am,' said the village gigolo, grinning.

'At last! Tell me, Petrus Son-of-God, am I your elder, or not?'

'What?' said the gigolo, and laughed. 'I don't quite get you.'

'Am I your elder, yes or no?'

'Oh, yes, yes, of course you are —'

'Was I not born some years before you?'

'Certainly, years and years before me, years before most if not all of us —'

'Excellent,' said Duckfoot Johnny. He seemed suddenly much more sober. 'In that case, tell me, don't you owe me obedience, on principle?'

'Yes, of course I do. What's the matter with you, though? What am I supposed to have done wrong now? What do I need to obey you over in particular?'

'Repeat after me,' said Duckfoot Johnny. '"St John of Kala, what do you command me to do if I want to go to heaven?" – Go on, say it.'

'St John of Kala,' repeated the gigolo, 'what do you command me to do if I want to go to heaven?'

'Excellent, Petrus Son-of-God, excellent. Here are two orders for you to execute faithfully. Faithfully, remember, or you won't go to heaven. In the first place — Go on, say after me, "In the first place" —'

'In the first place —'

'"" I must come running every time you summon me —"''

'I must come running every time you summon me —'

'"And as fast as possible," said Duckfoot Johnny, warming to his work. '"Faster than the accursed antelope which ravaged our young groundnut shoots last year."' The gigolo repeated each phrase as mechanically as if he had been in a catechism class.

'"In the second place, I must fill our guest's glass every time it is empty."'

The gigolo promised to do this, and echoed Duckfoot Johnny's 'Amen'.

'I bless you, my son,' Duckfoot Johnny concluded, 'in the name of the Father and the Son —' He pronounced the words with pleased emphasis, and sketched the gesture of benediction in an irresistibly comic parody of any missionary.

'Don't forget me if you want anyone baptized,' another young man remarked.

This young man was known as Abraham the Boneless Wonder: another nickname. Why Abraham rather than Moses or Nebuchadnezzar I had no idea; but the 'Boneless Wonder' was self-explanatory. Sitting or standing, walking or running, he showed himself more flexible than any normal vertebrate, let alone a human being, has any right to be. He behaved as though he was filleted.

'Ah, the Boneless Wonder!' said Duckfoot Johnny. 'How are you, dear boy? Didn't they ever teach you in catechism that anybody can administer baptism in an emergency, not just the priest?'

'Teach *me*? I did the teaching myself – to a crowd of kids when I was a school monitor. The most miserable period of my life. By the way, was all that rigmarole really necessary?'

'Certainly it was.' Duckfoot Johnny said, 'and no joke: our guest's glass was empty.'

'Oh, in that case I'll excuse you,' the Boneless Wonder observed, with a perfectly straight face.

Then they fell into each other's arms for a long embrace, muttering inarticulate nothings, their tongues heavy with drink. They were so tightly enlaced, and reeled about so much, that they nearly fell over on the beaten earth floor of the hut.

Then, when they had finished embracing each other, they sat down: Duckfoot Johnny on his stool, the Boneless Wonder on the ground at Johnny's feet. He still kept hold of Johnny, by the knees now.

'You have no idea how desperately I love you,' he said to Johnny, in a voice that fairly throbbed with emotion.

'Abraham, my brother,' Duckfoot Johnny replied, 'of course you love me: how could it be otherwise? So many of our friends are dead already; who knows when one of us will vanish likewise? And which of us will be the first to go? It may be tomorrow, for all we know. Do you remember Messi, Elias Messi I mean? We saw him putting up his rods and tackle for a month's fishing holiday up-river; we even saw him off down the other other end of the village, didn't we? Two days later he was done for: drowned. Poor Messi. If I didn't have you, God knows what sort of miserable life I should lead.'

'What about me? I hardly dare imagine life without your company. A few days, maybe, but for ever – ugh, please don't talk about such things. It's unlucky. Anyway, we shouldn't let our minds run on such morbid topics.'

'You're right, Abraham my brother; absolutely right.'

They never laughed once, either of them; vainly I scanned their faces for the least hint of humour during this odd exchange.

'You know,' Duckfoot Johnny said, turning to me, 'all the young people in this village really are brothers in a manner of speaking. We're all the grandchildren of the same man. He had about fifty wives, and never seems to have had any very clear idea of how many children he produced. He was a frightful chap, old Grandpa was.' He giggled delightedly. 'I never knew him, actually. But he was a holy terror, all right. Oh yes.'

Again there came that lunatic giggle. 'When he thundered, baobab trees would split in two from top to bottom, and great fires broke out in the sky, huge tongues of flame devouring heaven like the end of the world. The real thunder fell silent, like a gorilla, terrified by a more frightful voice than its own. Every living creature crawled into the bosom of the earth to hide from his rage; they tucked themselves away like people waiting for a flood to subside.

'He died one day through having killed one of his grand-children, a baby. He didn't do it on purpose; he wasn't the kind of man to kill his grandchildren deliberately. He simply wanted to punish a daughter-in-law of his who had offended him, and the woman happened to be carrying the baby in her arms. He touched the child quite accidentally, and died him-self the same evening.'

I was astonished. 'You mean he died without being ill?'

'Oh, he was ill all right; he had killed his own grandson.'

'But that isn't a *disease*,' I protested.

'Certainly it is; he died of it.'

Instinct told me not to pursue the matter further.

Petrus Son-of-God had only one job henceforward that evening: to keep an almost over-solicitous eye on my glass. Even when I forgot to drink for some time, the young man would come over to me and whisper in my ear: 'Come on, old fellow, drink up and let me give you another. Do you want to stop me getting into Heaven?'

He delivered this little speech in so grotesque a fashion that I had no alternative but to do as he requested; as a result I was becoming drunk myself, but slowly, and with dignity. The guitarist, I saw more clearly as the evening wore on, was a real artist. He thrummed away at his instrument indefatigably, changing his *tempo* every so often with effortless ease, and catching out the singers. When he sang himself, each song slid imperceptibly into the next. The dancing went on too, its staccato rhythm marked by hand-clapping like short practice bursts of machine-gun fire. Duckfoot Johnnie sat beside me and went on with his gossip regardless. I looked about for Zambo, but couldn't see him any longer.

Duckfoot Johnny, aware of my embarrassment, said: 'You're wondering what's become of your cousin, aren't you?

37

Don't worry; he's in excellent company, and he'll be back in a moment. He's the kind of fellow who can't get to sleep so long as there's a girl to screw somewhere in the world. They're both the same, him and Son-of-God, the old urge is too much for them. There's a girl giving them a lot of trouble at the moment because she doesn't want to play. A very odd creature. If you ask my opinion, she's abnormal. I've tried myself. So's everyone else. Not a hope. Never seen such a stuck-up little piece. Talk about putting on airs! Hard to see what she *does* want. I fancy I found out soon enough, though, between you and me. No one else has. I didn't press the point, anyway. Young creatures can be mulish as hell.'

There was a pause. Then he went on: 'See all these pretty little girls dancing? They all belong to our tribe, worse luck. Sometimes I wish I belonged to another tribe, just so's I could come over and screw 'em all. Plenty of fun for you, though. The town girls are pretty hot, aren't they?'

'Well,' I said, 'there are pretty ones and plain ones, the same as everywhere else —'

'Honoured guest —' Duckfoot Johnny began.

'My name is Medza. Jean-Marie Medza.'

'Very well then. Honoured Jean-Marie, do you want a girl? I can get you one this evening. Yes?'

'No, not this evening,' I said. 'I'm too exhausted. I've had to pedal all that way on my bike, up all the hills, too. I don't know if you realize how far it is.'

'That's all right; just as you like. Let's say tomorrow, then.'

'Oh – yes, perhaps – all right, tomorrow.' I must have had a most alarmingly hunted expression on my face.

'Tell me, Jean-Marie,' Duckfoot Johnny went on, 'we are pals, aren't we?'

'Of course we are.'

'Thank you, old chap. You're fond of pretty girls, I suppose?'

'Oh, ah – yes, like everyone else —'

'You've tickled a few up in the big city, too, haven't you? Come on, own up!'

'Nothing very much,' I muttered. 'One here, one there – no really big stuff —'

Was it the wine I had drunk which enabled me to lie so easily? Luckily Zambo returned just in time to rescue me from the purgatory through which Duckfoot Johnny was putting me. We said good-bye and left the party. By now I was in a decidedly nervous state.

When we got home we found that Zambo's parents had not only got home from the fields, but gone to bed. My cousin took me to a spare bedroom which was all ready for me, just as though they had been expecting a guest. (It turned out that they always had it ready for any visitor who might drop in.)

'Listen, little cousin,' Zambo said to me while I undressed, 'the best thing for you to do is to go to bed, and leave the old folk to sleep in peace. It makes no odds whether you see them now or tomorrow morning, except that they'll be in a better temper then. And as for the family of this woman you're here to find, I shouldn't hurry if I were you. I know that sort of little tart; she'll be off doing the rounds with all her old chums. We won't see her around these parts for a few days yet.'

So that was the explanation of the amused, ironic glance he had given me earlier on.

'Anyway, we'll go and have a talk with her father tomorrow. Don't worry your head too much about what to say to the family. I'll be there with you, and I know how to fix things. Oh, and it doesn't matter if you're feeling hungry, by the way; we'll have a tremendous breakfast tomorrow morning, a real feast.'

When he had shut the door and left me to my solitary thoughts, I decided that notwithstanding all he had said he was a dangerous customer. It also occurred to me that despite our physical dissimilarity, we nevertheless had something in common.

It was clear that my stay in Kala was going to last longer than I had at first supposed; but I had no regrets about having come. Once again I was beginning to persuade myself that, thanks to this unforeseen and at first unwelcome journey, I might experience here such adventures as I had never before imagined. Duckfoot Johnny, for example, had already promised me a girl for tomorrow. . . .

The first day I spent at Kala – the day after my arrival, that is – nothing of particular importance took place.

Very early in the morning my cousin Zambo came and woke me up, saying that his father was asking to see me. My uncle turned out to be as tall as his son – this, indeed, I had already observed from the photographs pinned up in the dining-room – but he was of a different build. His torso and shoulders were heavy enough, but they tapered away into thin legs and (for a peasant) decidedly small feet. He wore a perpetual frown, and worked his jaws nervously, as though he were constantly pursuing some complicated idea. Come to think of it, I never saw him completely idle. If he wasn't thinking, or listening to someone talking, he at least kept his hands busy with some small physical task – sharpening his machete on a stone, mending a lock, pruning an orange-tree that stood behind his bungalow, and heaven knows what else.

He was a man of few words, so taciturn, indeed, that at times he gave the impression of being dumb. He laughed even more seldom than he talked. He was a really odd creature – so odd, indeed, that at times I wondered whether he was not a stranger by origin, some wanderer who had happened to settle here. He was utterly different from the general run of his neighbours.

That first occasion, as soon as I had wished him good morning, he merely grunted 'How d'you do, young fellow?' and said not a word more. That was that.

His wife was nearly as tall as he was. As a young girl she must have been stunning; but repeated pregnancies, and long hours of work in field or cocoa-plantation, had left their mark on her. She was gentle, charming, eager to be of help, and as humble as a saint. She too was remarkably taciturn – probably by reason of that imitative tendency which, they say, is common in long-established relationships.

How old they were it was hard to tell. She must have been quite young, in fact, and preserved some traces of her youth. Like all the girls of my mother's generation, she must have been married off at puberty – about fifteen, perhaps even younger. As her eldest son was nearly twenty, she could hardly be more than thirty-five or so herself. Her husband had obviously knocked about the world a good deal: he even spoke a few words of German, as nearly with the correct accent as made no difference. He must be at least fifty, I reckoned, but he didn't look it. In fact, he appeared peculiarly ageless, in a way that suggested lack of interest in such problems. What *he* was more concerned with was still being strong enough to work: a somewhat superfluous worry. By the look of him he had ten or twenty good years ahead still.

My uncle, my cousin, and I had an early breakfast together. (The women ate in the kitchen.) Afterwards, the old couple went off to the fields. Zambo did not accompany them. His job, as a rule, was to work in the family cocoa-patch. This, like all family cocoa-patches, was close to the village. On the other hand, everything cultivated as food – ground-nuts, yams, bananas, manioc, and the rest – was planted as far away as possible to leave room for the cocoa-plantations to be extended.

I had ample opportunity to watch the field-workers, who were early risers, squatting on their verandas washing, eating their scanty breakfast, getting their things together, and trailing off into the forest on their way to work. The only ones left behind were the babies, and a few slightly older children to look after them.

Before leaving, the friends I had made the evening before came to pay their respects and ask if I had slept well. They were sober now, and they examined me with a fresh curiosity, as if we were meeting all over again for the first time. They only cracked an occasional joke, and there were almost no obscenities.

The sun had been up for several hours when Zambo took me to see Niam's father-in-law. Brisk and keen-minded, with no signs of infirmity and great agility in conversation, this father-in-law was, nevertheless, a very old man, and no longer went to work. He sat on a bamboo bed, and his hut was full of smoke. He seemed very much at his ease. It was Zambo who told him who I was, and why I had come to Kala.

The old man gave me a casual glance only, and then asked had his son-in-law not sent him anything? I answered that Niam had given me no kind of present to deliver, but that this must have been due to mere forgetfulness on his part. The old man looked highly surprised, but didn't press the point, as though the present was of only secondary importance to him. Then he sat for some time in silence, his arms folded and resting on his knees, while he stared through the narrow doorway into the sunlight outside.

At last he said: 'Look, youngster, this business isn't really my concern at all, but my daughter's. She's away at the present, but she'll certainly be back in a few days. You must discuss everything with her. I married her off a long time ago, and never gave it a thought afterwards. Therefore it's up to her to decide whether she returns to her husband or not.'

'But she has no choice —' Zambo began, with a fine show of scandalized righteousness.

The old man smiled.

'Listen to the boy talking,' he observed. 'Very moral. But you're young, you've been to school, haven't you? Don't you know that the Whites passed a divorce-law some time back?'

'You mean,' Zambo persisted, 'that you'd be ready to back your daughter if she wanted to obtain a divorce? I presume you have enough means to repay her dowry, then?'

The old man smiled again, completely unruffled.

'My boy, it may be that I'm not over-rich. To tell the truth, I'm pretty poor. But if my daughter really is sick of her husband, I'd help her in any way I could if it came to the pinch.'

'Yes, of course, very creditable,' Zambo muttered, and at once began to get up as if to go.

I had often heard of discussions being 'broken off'; it occurred to me at this moment that I had just seen a good example of the process with my own eyes. But at once, to my great disappointment, the old man added: 'Listen, boy: I didn't say for certain that my daughter wanted a divorce. To be quite honest, I don't know what her intentions are. If we're to get to the bottom of the affair, we'd better wait.'

'Fine, fine,' Zambo said.

We went out, with an air of dignity and apparent good conscience, rather like the envoys of a Great Power against which some one-horse country has rashly declared war.

'The dirty swine!' Zambo exploded, as soon as we were out of earshot.

We idled the rest of the morning away. My cousin kept firing questions at me, and I gave him rather distracted answers. I was racking my brains for some good excuse to elude Duckfoot Johnny's highly questionable proposals.

Early in the afternoon the young folk began to straggle back to the village; they never worked very long hours. They carried bundles of sugar-cane, and took pleasure (they said) in making a present of it to the town's guest – meaning me.

They then proposed that we should go for a swim: the proposal was carried unanimously, with only one abstention – me. I don't happen to be able to swim. All the same, I went with them.

It was a broad stream, almost a full-sized river. They all stripped off in a flash and plunged into the water stark naked. At first I said I didn't think I would bathe. They insisted on my coming in with them, jollying me along, even saying that if I still refused they'd haul me in by main force. I knew they were only joking and wouldn't really do it. Nevertheless I took off all my clothes, except a pair of brief pants. At the moment I entered the water – still wearing my pants – they all burst into shrieks of laughter.

'Why don't you undress properly?' Zambo asked.

'You haven't got a dose by any chance, have you?' inquired the Boneless Wonder.

'Perhaps it's a real whopper and he doesn't want to show us,' giggled Son-of-God.

43

'Or a tiny shrimp of a thing.' This from Duckfoot Johnny, who was laughing himself sick.

'Him?' someone else said. 'Don't be funny. I bet it's twice as big as yours. I know these chaps from the city.'

My patience was exhausted by these jokes at my expense; despite the unspeakable shame they produced in me, I took the hint and stripped off to the buff. At once a chorus of admiring gasps went up.

'Lordy, Son-of-God was right!'

'You can say that again!'

'Look at it – colossal!'

At once there was a kind of competition to see who had the biggest. They all came out of the water and inspected each other with great care. Finally Duckfoot Johnny announced that, without question, the *smallest* was, as always, Son-of-God's.

'Hopeless, hopeless,' he said. 'Won't it *ever* grow? I'll tell you a good dodge, though. Get yourself bitten by one of these black ants. It'll swell up to double, no, three times the size in a flash, believe you me.'

'The trouble is,' someone said thoughtfully, 'that it'll go down again.'

'Or die altogether,' put in someone else.

'Poor Son-of-God.'

'You don't know what you're talking about,' Son-of-God said at length, indignantly. 'It may *look* small at the moment, but that's because of the cold water, I remember times when it grew as long as a banana-snake and as thick as a python—'

'You horrible liar,' said Duckfoot Johnny. 'You never do anything but boast.'

'All right, then,' Son-of-God said, 'we'll make a little experiment. Lend me your girl-friend just for one night. I bet you anything you like she won't have anything to do with you any more afterwards.'

Everyone burst out laughing.

'What instrument, then, in *your* opinion,' Son-of-God went

on cheerfully, 'did I use to get Bikoé's and Tsala's girls, not to mention all the rest?'

'I know you and your dirty little tricks,' Duckfoot Johnny replied. 'You cheat – you play unfair —'

'Give me an instance.'

'Certainly. You rub your whatsit with lemon-peel, for a start. *And* you eat all sorts of herbs and roots to tone yourself up. You learnt all these little wrinkles from your uncles – your *maternal* uncles, of course. Disgusting old men they are.'

They all giggled at this, and then plunged back into the water again. I envied them their effortless capacity to swim; and, indeed, they would have gone on swimming for the rest of the day if they had not been interrupted about five in the afternoon – just as the sun was beginning to go down – by a voice from behind the nearest thicket. It broke the spell.

'You *men*!' said the voice (which was high and fluting and obviously belonged to a girl), 'you spend the whole day *pigging* it in there and never give a thought to your sisters. Come on, out of the water with you; it's our turn now. Hurry up!'

The boys dug their toes in.

'Go and swim somewhere else,' they shouted. 'Go and find some other creek.'

'Where?'

'That's up to you. There's sure to be places where you can bathe as long as you like. This is the men's pool.'

At this point the boys went into a huddle, and the same spokesman added: 'If Eliza's there, tell her to come and swim with us. Tell her not to be afraid – we won't do her any harm. We'll even cover up our you-know-whats —'

Hoots of laughter on both sides. Then the girl's piping voice said: 'All right, you nasty boys. If you won't, you won't. We'll just have to finish somewhere else. We know a nice pool upstream from here. That's where we'll go.'

'Where do you mean?'

'Upstream, I told you. Got it?'

The word 'upstream' produced results as if by magic. The

boys all scrambled out of the water, their faces wrinkled up as if in disgust.

Duckfoot Johnny swore angrily. 'Women upstream and us down here!' he exclaimed, 'there are limits —' He spat.

We dressed quickly. The girls saw that we were out of the water, and came closer.

'Off with you!' they screeched. 'What are you hanging about for? Want to peep at us undressing, eh?'

'We want Eliza!' the wag declared. 'Where is she, the gorgeous little thing?'

'What do you want with her?'

'A bit of all right, eh, chaps?'

'What – all of you together?'

'Oh no; we'll queue up.'

The girls burst into rather scandalized giggles.

'You can see Eliza isn't here,' one of them said at length.

'Where's she gone, then?'

'She's run away and hidden in the jungle. Go on, hop it, the lot of you.'

Finally a girl made as if to undress, and at once all the boys scampered off. I followed them.

We were hardly out of sight among the bushes when the girls began to shout: 'Leave us the young boy from the town – come on, let's be having him!'

'Don't be impatient,' one of the gang called back, 'you'll find him in the village soon enough, ready and waiting. All you have to do is to work out who has him which night and let him know.'

I don't know how I managed it, but I succeeded in avoiding all Duckfoot Johnny's little schemes to get me into bed with a girl. Perhaps he let the matter drop, I can't remember; he may have forgotten his suggestions of the previous night, or had some other reason for changing his mind.

To the best of my recollection, the day after this memorable swimming-party was a Sunday. On Sunday neither my uncle nor anyone else worked in the fields, so plenty of people kept dropping in to see us – or rather, to see my uncle – not all together, but one after another. Each one insisted on seeing me, and shaking hands; I complied with their requests without understanding what it was all about. As a guest, I took care not to criticize their curiosity, but it made my cousin Zambo surprisingly cross. He was (as I now realize) beginning to have certain personal designs on me which he could hardly carry out while I was continually monopolized by inquisitive visitors.

In a word, I could see quite clearly that I was being lionized. Everyone in the village was paying court to me, especially my uncle, who went to great and obvious trouble to do me little services. He showed me a good deal more respect than an elderly man should do to a youth – certainly more than was sanctioned by custom. Yet, unlike the usual unkind comments which such behaviour normally provokes, in this case nothing at all was said by those who came to the house. Everyone seemed to think it was a favour simply to talk with me. As soon as I realized this I got into an agony of embarrassment.

I had become a kind of universal pet or mascot for the whole of Kala: not only a strange animal, but an animal that they liked to examine at close quarters, and hear roar, or howl, or bray, or whatever. The women used to turn up in droves, too, and look me over with that greedy up-and-down stripping expression common to women the world over. Never in my life have I been examined so minutely or with so little shame.

In the afternoon one woman, hardly bothering to conceal her feelings, put her cards – more or less – on the table.

'Young man,' she said, 'you shouldn't take offence at people being so interested in you. We don't see a college-educated boy like you here every day of the week – *and* a city-dweller into the bargain!'

Heavens, I had forgotten that. Educated *and* a city-dweller. She's right, damn it, I thought, after a moment's stunned silence. As an educated city-boy, my uppermost thought was that I had made a stupid nonsense of my exams. But never mind; a diploma, even by default, was a rare enough commodity in the Kala market. So that was it: educated *and* a city-dweller. Why hadn't I thought of it earlier?

Now the woman began to ask me questions. She was about the same age as my mother, but prematurely aged by the heavy manual labour which all these up-country people undertake.

'What do they teach you at school?' she demanded.

'Who?'

'The Whites, of course, boy! What do they teach you?'

The room was crowded, so I couldn't laugh, which was what I wanted to do.

'What do they teach me? Oh, heaps of things,' I said, unconvincingly.

The whole thing embarrassed me horribly. I wanted to be kind to this woman; she meant well enough; but how on earth was I to give her the most elementary notion of such things as geography, advanced mathematics or the social sciences? Nevertheless, I had a shot at it; with gestures and stumbling, awkward vague phrases I did my best.

Her one desire was to keep me well-disposed towards her, willing to oblige.

'Come and see us one of these evenings,' she suggested finally. 'We'd be delighted to see you, my husband and I. My husband admires you enormously, you know. He's sworn by you for the last two days. Come and visit us one night soon and bring your uncle with you.'

My uncle, who was listening to this conversation, smiled with a satisfaction that took me somewhat aback. For my own part I didn't take this invitation very seriously; I honestly believed that the old lady was suffering from the effects of senility. I changed my mind about this a few days later.

Gradually the conviction was forming in me that these apparently unimportant incidents would play a part in my life out of all proportion to their present slight significance; that they would, indeed, mark a turning-point in my life. I am not only thinking of what had already happened since my arrival, but what was yet to come: I was convinced, even then, that there *was* more – much more – to come.

I may perhaps be deluding myself in this belief. It is easy, after all, to tell yourself afterwards that you sensed in advance just what effect some moment – or even a longer period – would have on your subsequent life, even the exact tone and colour it would produce. All the same, I remember having had a similar kind of presentiment on several previous occasions; and every time it turned out just as I expected.

When I was a little boy, I had been playing in the streets of Vimili one day with other boys about my own age. Full of cheerful bounce, we went scampering past the hospital. Right opposite this hospital, on the other side of the road, a convict gang was pulling down some clay-brick buildings under military supervision. The buildings were badly constructed – too narrow and far too high – and were being demolished for their material. It was a dangerous job for workers who lacked both experience and proper equipment – country boys, most of them, who might have been gaoled only the week before.

They were using heavy balks of timber as battering-rams. Since they had no ladders, they attacked the walls at ground level, knocking hole after hole through the clay till the entire wall came crashing down.

We found them busy demolishing a building even taller and narrower than the rest. As soon as I took in the spectacle of these young boys toiling away with their rams against that puddled clay wall, I was struck all of a heap; I stood there, petrified, rooted to the spot. In this instant – despite the tumbled ruins on either side, which suggested that the prisoners had already demolished several other houses unharmed – I knew that something terrible was going to happen, something so serious that I would never forget it if I saw it. My friends first tried to drag me away, then gave up and stayed there with me.

As the work went on, a horrible, impalpable fear rose and spread throughout my entire being. It was akin to the feeling you get when you are reading a detective story written by a cold, sadistic author, expert at twisting the last drop of suspense and horror out of his material. The walls were intact on the upper floors, but grew steadily weaker at their foundations The beaten earth flaked away, revealing a core of puddled clay bricks. The whole building looked like a giant who was having the flesh torn from his bones, leaving only a huge skeleton behind. Suddenly the guards shouted to the prisoners: 'Look out! Get away, quick!' The edifice was collapsing. The prisoners darted away into the courtyard, bounding like bull-frogs. It all happened in a flash. The walls came down with a dull roar and and a crash; and instantly we heard the in-describable shriek of a trapped animal. One of the men had not got clear in time.

I saw the hideously mangled body, when they dragged it out from the great lumps of rubble, and that was an unpleasant enough sight, in all conscience. But what sticks in my memory, what I shall never forget as long as I live – especially when I witness any accident, or any more than momentary demon-stration of unhappiness – is that shriek of a trapped man, calling out (or trying to) not so much for help as in protest against the whole ghastly injustice of life. That cry of mingled agony and defiance will always ring in my ears like some obsessional hallucination.

Another time, I was on holiday at my maternal uncle's, and had gone rambling in the forest with some other boys, when we heard a very queer bird-call, repeated again and again. I knew that bird; it was the one we call the Ghost's Daughter, or some such name, and it wasn't the first time I had run into it. Its call came from a thicket quite close to us: it began very suddenly, a deathly sad noise, dripping with nostalgia, just as if it had been laid on specially for us – as if it was somehow *connected* with us.

It was a smooth, unwavering melody, rather like a river in its reaches below a weir: every note was low-pitched, with a calm implacable fatalism in its timbre that penetrated to my inmost soul (rather like the soap enemas I was given in my sickly childhood), and long-drawn-out emphasis on the final note of each phrase. It sounded as though this bird knew very well that its song symbolized some person's destiny; and also –

so detached was the tone, so emotionally indifferent – that the knowledge left it totally unmoved. It was simply an anonymous messenger.

Without saying a word, we all fell silent, listening to the bird. When it had finished singing, my cousins began talking and laughing again as though nothing had happened. But I felt differently: from that very moment I was absolutely certain I should never forget this encounter with the Ghost's Daughter. That evening I learnt that one of my younger sisters was dead.

In the same way, for equally inexplicable reasons, I was now sure that I would remember my visit to Kala for the rest of my life: I could sense the cause without yet being able to bring it into the daylight.

Every evening, as the sun went down, the distinct features of village and surrounding forest merged in dark anonymity, and night spread across the sky like a great velvet cloth, yet scarcely more sombre than the tropical undergrowth which it obscured. And every evening, watching this metamorphosis, I thought: Look your fill. A darkening picture, perhaps; but look closely, you cannot risk forgetting it. When you remember it in after time, think of your pleasure at recalling every minutest detail, even the infinite gradations of shading in the evening sky, or the bird in the distant forest, sadly celebrating the faithlessness of each fickle day, like a boy weeping for his mother's death. Think of the grey, neutral banana-trees, their sharp outlines melting into the darkness till they take on the semblance of ghosts. Think, last, of the moon, rising in splendid self-annunciation behind the tangled trees, unlooked-for and incredible, slowly climbing till she rode clear at last, tranquil as a goddess, gleaming, radiant.

My real story began on the fourth day of my visit to Kala.

Niam's wife had still not showed up. Zambo and I had gone to see her father the evening before. The old man had taken the same line as he did during our first visit. It was a long time since he'd married off his daughter, he repeated, and he hadn't given it a thought since, make no mistake about that.

Anything that had happened since was hardly his concern. Anyway, was his daughter *expecting* me to come on this errand? Was it his fault if she'd gone off for a little open-air holiday.

No, it was hardly his fault. But why did he talk as though he were on the witness-stand in court?

Zambo replied, in much the same tone: 'A little holiday, perhaps. But are you sure about it being an *open-air* holiday?'

The old man took no notice of Zambo's remark. He put on the expression of an adulterous wife who has just been asked by her husband who she is deceiving him with, and prefers to turn a deaf ear to such questions.

On the morning of the fourth day after my arrival in Kala, I had two very interesting discussions: one with my cousin, the other with my uncle.

Zambo came into my room very early, before I was even up. I used to enjoy watching him while we talked, and studying his various facial expressions. He was a real case; I have never seen a man who presented such a contrast between mind and body. Outwardly he was the epitome of brute strength; but in this tough frame lurked an oddly mild and humble disposition. His humility would have done credit to some Hindu ascetic, who had endured all those disciplines designed to mortify the flesh in the pursuit of true saintliness.

On this occasion, unluckily, it was still dark in my bedroom and I had no chance to observe his expression. Even after he opened the window he sat with his back to the light. I can't help feeling I missed a most enlightening spectacle; but in fact it was quite impossible to see how this young Greek demi-god looked as he unfolded his queer proposition.

'Still asleep?' he inquired as he sat down.

Certainly I was still asleep. This was meant to be a holiday. The whole atmosphere of Kala was soporific, if it came to that. I didn't answer my cousin; I simply stretched and grunted in a friendly way, to make him understand that his presence in no way disturbed me. Being the kind of fellow he was, he might have worried about this.

He sounded very tired, and I decided he must have spent all night making love with his mistress or some casual pick-up – certainly he had vanished very early the previous evening. He paused for a while, coughing and clearing his throat.

'H'r'm!' he said at length, 'you're in luck. Wouldn't mind being in your place myself.'

This was funny; at that moment I would have given anything to be in his. I screwed up my eyes, trying to make out his face in the half-light. But I could get only a vague impression of its more noticeable features: Zambo was extremely tall, even when seated. For my money he was good-looking, too. But why had he come out with this remark? Was he being sarcastic, by any chance? I suddenly distrusted him: people who look stupid are generally sharper than one supposes. Unfortunately, however, he was absolutely sincere.

'What makes you say that?' I asked pleasantly.

'Oh, plenty of reasons.' He stopped, searching for words. He was really beginning to surprise me.

'Plenty of reasons, perhaps,' I said patiently, 'but what are they? Come on, tell. I'm dying to know.'

His very hesitation gave him away. To tell the truth, he had already sounded me several times on the question. I had always heard him out a little coldly – not that his suggestions left me indifferent, but in this particular field I was still a long way behind him. He was convinced that I despised what he had to offer; it would never have occurred to him that my hesitation might spring from shame or timidity, especially since I was a city-boy. Me, a city slicker: just imagine it!

All the same, I couldn't bring myself to fall in with his plans. I decided to get myself out of this fix just as I had with Duckfoot Johnny on the day of my arrival – by careful evasions, which would, as far as possible, save my face, besides defending the good reputation of city-dwellers. What a fool I was! Why didn't I simply ask my obliging cousin for some practical hints and face the unknown squarely? It wasn't as if I didn't *want* it; every drop of hot blood in my veins cried out in desire, and long years spent over books had not succeeded in crushing my natural urges.

'It's a girl,' he said.

A pause.

'She's simply dying for you.'

Good. This was it at last.

'Are you joking?' I asked, without much conviction.

'Get away with you, you know all the girls are mad about you. Why pretend not to see it? You ought to be pleased.'

'Girls mad about *me*? What about you? I bet one glance at your torso is enough to get them into a real state —'

I spoke lightly enough, and (I admit) with a certain degree of exaggeration: but I honestly believed that a Tarzan such as my cousin could hardly fail to impress any woman. This psychological *naïveté* annoyed my cousin considerably, and he took my little joke very ill.

'I'm all right, thank you very much,' he snapped.

What, I thought, *another* complex? I had already uncovered two or three. Basically, Zambo was going up in my estimation. He was not so stupid as he seemed. A man with complexes, I argued, must have a rich emotional life. I was beginning to feel my way towards a revised estimate of his personality.

'Fine, fine,' I said, in a conciliatory voice. 'Let's take one thing at a time. The girl is pretty, I gather —'

'Pretty? She's wonderful. I doubt whether there's a girl to equal her even in the city.'

'That's something, anyway. Now – you say she's dying for me. Tell me, where's the poor thing managed to see me, if – as you say – she likes me so much?'

'You *are* a funny customer. Do you imagine people haven't had a good look at you ever since you got here?'

He paused again, then went on: 'Tell me, honestly, don't you get a kick out of a girl like that wanting you so much? If you only knew how gorgeous she is! I'll tell you something else – she's from another district, she doesn't belong here. Since she's been in the village everyone's been round her like flies, they've tried everything. But it's no good, she turned them all down. She turned *us* all down, do you get it? You're the only one she wants, and you don't even care!'

I cared all right. I was shocked at how much I cared. That made it pretty clear to me that this girl wouldn't leave me indifferent when it came to the point. Lovely and disdainful, was she? We should see.

Zambo's persistence was, nevertheless, becoming a little irksome. It was as though he had convinced himself that I was bursting to go to bed with a woman – which was true enough. It hinted at the invaluable service he had done me in acting as go-between; that, too, I admitted. But above all I got the feeling that he had made it a point of honour to get me to say yes to this particular girl, and no other. This last consideration aroused my suspicions. If it was true, *why* this girl in particular? Why not some other? If only I had a bit more nerve, I thought, I'd ask him to lay on one of his girl cousins, a local. This other girl was outside the tribe, and fair pickings for the young gallants of Kala; if I had a mind to a girl, I had the whole tribe to choose from. *Up to you*, Duckfoot Johnny had said.

'When did she say she liked me?' I asked, for want of anything better to say.

He had met her the night before; there had been dancing going on at the other end of the village. Very smoothly, she had plied him with questions: what was his cousin's name, dozens of other details about him. It was quite clear to him that this girl was interested in me.

'A girl doesn't go asking questions like that about a chap for nothing,' he said.

At this point, apparently, he had asked her straight out whether she fancied his cousin. She hadn't said no; in fact, she had made no answer at all. But as she didn't say no, that meant she would have said yes if she *had* answered. Girls never say yes straight away; besides, there are precious few of them who ever say yes, unequivocally, at all. In the normal way they simply surrender. She had given herself away, too, in a manner of speaking, since a moment later she had remarked that she would like a closer glimpse of this cousin of his – a more than significant remark. She was, he concluded, coming round to the house that evening after dinner, between seven and eight.

'All we have to do now is wait. Father won't hang around in the way. She's been round several times already listening to records. There's one special favourite of hers we've got. That'll be her excuse this evening. We'll talk while the gramophone's playing.'

That suited me fine.

It had only needed a normally choosy girl to make advances to me, and my self-confidence got a tremendous fillip. I was dreaming of her already, mad about her. All the same, I was pretty scared too. What on earth was I going to do to make her love me more? What ought I to say? There was something else, too. The girl had made advances to me; that meant she knew all about the business. She must have had masses more experience than I had.

Suddenly I remembered what my elder brother used to din sadistically into my brain: 'Old boy,' he would say, 'anyone who's still a virgin at your age ought to start on an emancipated city-girl; it's the only way of making up for lost time quickly enough. You learn the lot at one go. All the same,' he added quickly, 'you've got to really satisfy her – and she must be a kindly woman. Otherwise she'd make such fool of you that you'd never dare look at a woman again for the rest of your life, if I know you.'

'Well, what's she like?' I asked Zambo, in some agitation.

'I've already told you: she's pretty, extremely pretty. Wait till this evening; you'll see for yourself.'

I felt sorry for him. But he could at least try to understand what I was trying to say, I thought. Undaunted, I tackled the question from another angle.

'Is she young?' I inquired.

'Oh yes, very young: she hasn't had a child yet.'

'Look,' I said, 'you can get to a ripe old age without having any children.'

'I tell you she's *young*; she isn't even married.'

This was more encouraging. If the girl was all that attractive, and her parents hadn't yet married her off, it could only be because they judged her too young still. Yet even if my cousin had managed to work out what was worrying me, could he have given me any clear-cut answer? If he couldn't get off with the girl himself, he obviously didn't know her all that well.

'Right, then,' he said, 'we won't go out this evening, agreed? We'll stay in and wait for her.'

'Of course,' I replied. 'That's O.K. by me.'

I was reckoning on finding some way of escape; it was even conceivable that Zambo might pull my chestnuts out of the fire for me himself. Unfortunately I had no grounds for such a suspicion; I knew very well that my cousin had far too strong a sense of loyalty to try anything like that.

At this point we were called in to breakfast.

This was, according to local custom, an enormous meal, chiefly because they only had two meals a day. The women went to work in the fields early in the morning, and only returned late in the afternoon. The children and those few men left in the village fed themselves on bananas, eggs, yams, roasted ground-nuts, and other such things. It never occurred to any of the men to cook a proper meal for themselves.

The table was loaded with food. My uncle was distinctly lacking in table manners: he crammed his mouth so full that a great bulge appeared in each cheek, and I was afraid he might burst. I trained myself not to catch his eye during meals, so as to avoid betraying my astonishment at his feeding habits. His son, on the other hand, shot constant glances of shame and reproach at him. When my uncle noticed these grimaces, he stared back in dour astonishment and said: 'What's got into you? Do you normally gawp at folks like that when they're eating?'

Then he shrugged, and his jaws began their rhythmic champing once more. At one point he dumped a large leg of chicken on my plate and said: 'You don't eat enough, boy. Don't tell me the Whites teach you to starve yourself?'

I could never believe he meant this kind of question seriously. But he was determined to get a reply out of me. Like all taciturn men, when he did open his mouth he was determined to get proper attention. He repeated his question.

'No,' I said, 'it's just that I'm not in the habit of eating a lot.'

'That explains why you haven't grown as tall as you should, or put on enough weight. You ought to eat much more, boy.'

Zambo, at the end of the table, just managed to choke back a great snort of laughter.

'As for you,' his father observed with some severity, 'you'll never be anything but an imbecile. Look at your cousin here; he's younger than you, and he's really got somewhere already.'

'Not everyone can be like him,' my cousin replied ironically. 'If I went off and got my diploma, who'd do the work in our cocoa-plantation?'

'For all the work you do there,' his father retorted, 'you might as well be a student and have done with it.'

'Suits me. I shan't go up there any more in that case.'

'Well, well,' said my uncle. 'I suppose you think I'm going to drop dead this evening, eh? Then from tomorrow you'll be able to do as you please.'

'I give up,' Zambo burst out, laughing. '*You* just said I didn't do any work in the plantation, so there's no point in my going there, surely?'

'I ask you,' my uncle said to me. 'Just look at this great booby of mine.'

In fact, underneath all this chaffing, they got on extremely well together. If I'd ever answered my father back as Zambo did, I don't know what would have happened; but I'm pretty sure I wouldn't have forgotten the occasion.

If only they wouldn't treat me just as a 'scholar' and nothing else! I'd have given all the diplomas in the world to swim like Duckfoot Johnny, or dance like the Boneless Wonder, or have the sexual experience of Petrus Son-of-God, or throw an assegai like Zambo. I wanted desperately to eat, drink, and be happy without having to bother my head about next term, or such depressing things as revision-work and orals. The very least I could do was to conquer my fear of women – even divorcées. I would soon learn how to respond to their advances. I would make up to this girl who was gone on me. I was forgetting, however, that afterwards there would be no reason for her to go on pining for me.

My uncle stretched out his neck, rather like an ostrich, and gulped down an enormous mouthful of food. He then blinked several times, filled himself a glass of water, and swallowed that too. Finally he cleared his throat and said: 'My boy,' (it was still quite an effort to articulate clearly) 'this evening we shall visit the woman who invited you to call the other day. We shall in all probability have dinner with her. We shall go round tonight about six o'clock.'

'Father,' said Zambo, in a worried voice, 'couldn't we possibly put off this visit for another day?'

'Why?' asked my uncle, astonished. 'Why on earth should you want it put off?'

'Oh, nothing. I just thought my young cousin might still be tired – and after all, there's plenty of time left for paying calls —'

'Who asked your opinion, anyway?' my uncle said, unanswerably. Then he turned to me. 'My boy,' he repeated firmly, 'we are going to call on this lady *tonight*. We have to go. She would be most hurt if we didn't.'

As you will have gathered, conversation between me and my uncle was of a somewhat limited nature, and a rather one-sided affair at that. I could, of course, have made up some kind of excuse; but people with a disability or dislike for talking have a natural inclination towards dictatorial behaviour. Besides, he had treated me with great kindness and consideration during my stay – for instance, had he not fed me on nothing but chicken since my arrival? But despite all these extenuating circumstances, I would rather he had *asked* me what day I would like to call on this woman, and not (to use the diplomatic cant phrase) taken a unilateral decision. Above all, he had picked on a most inopportune moment, and I resented this fiercely: I suddenly saw my hopes of meeting my mysterious beauty vanish into smoke. Curiously enough, my fear of actually being brought into contact with her disappeared in the same instant. (I could hardly hope to meet her now on that evening; she was working in the fields, and would not be back in the village till late in the afternoon. It would not be possible, I thought, to arrange another meeting.) All that remained was an inquisitive itch and that vague, diffuse kind of desire which all virgins experience, and which normally goes with curiosity.

'Perhaps this visit won't last long,' Zambo suggested when we were alone. 'Perhaps there'll be time to see her after all?'

Naturally his hope was not fulfilled, and I don't suppose he expected that it would be. He knew the customs of his own village perfectly well, and must have been aware that the only difficulty with visits of this kind was to end them.

'Are there many White children at your school?' my hostess inquired.

I said yes, there were a lot.

'More White than Coloured?'

'No; not nearly so many.'

'What are they *like*, these White children? Tell us what they're like,' she persisted.

'Heavens – just like children anywhere, the world over —'

'*Really?* Just like ordinary children?'

'Exactly,' I said. 'They have rows, and fights, and are insubordinate – there's no difference at all.'

A man's voice broke in. 'And in class,' he said, loudly. 'Are they cleverer than you in class?'

'No. They aren't either more clever or more stupid than we are. They're just the same as – as – a mixed bunch.'

'Will the learned gentleman please explain, then,' the same voice went on, in astonished tones, 'how it is that their minds work faster than ours?'

'They don't. They grasp a point no faster and no slower than we do.'

60

'Well, well. That's really surprising. They *ought* to be quicker in the uptake, though, oughtn't they?'

'Why should they?' another man's voice broke in. 'Why are you so determined that they should be quicker than our children? We don't breed young animals, do we? What are you thinking of?'

'How can you ask such a question?' the first man replied. 'It's perfectly reasonable to suppose that White children should learn faster than Black. What are they being taught? *Their* ancestral wisdom, not ours, isn't that so? Who invented aeroplanes and trains and cars and steamships? The Whites. Very well, then. Now if it was *our* ancestral wisdom that was taught in this school, it would be normal to expect Coloured children to learn faster than Whites, wouldn't it?'

The company were divided over this question, which provoked several fine displays of rhetoric, not least from the women. The argument went on till the man who had opposed this ingenious theory – having, to judge by the peremptory fashion in which he called the room to silence, thought up a superb and irrefutable gambit – now declared brusquely: 'Listen to me, all of you. Here's my personal opinion, for what it's worth. It's by no means certain that it *was* the Whites who invented cars and aeroplanes and all that. When you talk about Coloured folk, you mean us, don't you? All right, we're nobodies. But what about all the other Coloured peoples, all over the world? How can you be sure that *they* don't make planes and trains and cars?'

To judge by the approving murmur which greeted it, this argument was a popular one. Finally the first man admitted that its proposer was probably right, yes, he might very well be right.

I had not joined in the discussion at all, never having asked myself such questions before. All the same, I wanted to tell them that it wasn't true, that no Coloured people in the world manufactured aeroplanes. But I held my tongue. I should have had to explain too much else to them at the same time. What was more, my skill as a lecturer was, to say the least, debatable. They would not, in all likelihood, have understood me; and, worst of all, if they did it would probably give them a complex. On the whole I preferred them innocent of complexes. It struck me that colonialism had given them quite enough of such kinks already, without some dim compatriot of theirs adding yet more through sheer maladroitness. It was, so to speak, a concession to my public; and I don't, even today, regret it.

They seemed to have no immediate inclination to let me go. I could hardly leave by myself; it would have been the worst possible thing I could have done. To begin with, they had sat me down to a meal, a really gargantaun affair. Afterwards I waited to hear them tell me that it was all over, I could go home, they'd just asked me for the meal. That's how it would have been done at home if we were entertaining a casual stranger. But things were different here.

Scarcely was dinner over when my hostess began to fire a whole fusillade of questions at me. She sat next to me and went on absolutely ruthlessly, dragging detailed explanations out of me, and going back over muddled points with a needle-sharp clarity. She obviously was aware of all my weaknesses and shortcomings; she was equipped to give me the most humiliating oral I had ever been through in my life. To think that there are people like me whose job is passing exams all their life.

Then they all got down to it, and interrogated me non-stop. As there was a great number of them, they were often all asking me questions at once. This embarrassed me horribly, because I didn't know which ones to answer first: they varied in subject, but were all of equal interest. I was utterly disconcerted, and one thing embarrassed me in particular: the attitude of the women and young girls. They absolutely devoured me with their eyes, and the expressions they wore were so unequivocal that I could not help recognizing them for what they were at once, despite my natural modesty. It was like reading a young peasant girl's passionate love-letter.

Sometimes I glanced at Zambo, who squatted in a corner

miserably, indifferent to the atmosphere of enthusiasm permeating the room, perhaps even hating it, but in any case the disregarded odd man out. Occasionally I caught my uncle's eye, too; he looked strangely complacent, rather like an old French peasant who has just married off his daughter to the richest, best-looking young man in the district. He was gay and pleased, and obviously willing me to make a success of the occasion.

But I was thinking that I shouldn't see Eliza (that, I found out, was her name); not tonight, anyway, I told myself. Looking back, I suspect Eliza had become my symbol of absolute liberty, the freedom enjoyed by country boys like Duckfoot Johnny, the Boneless Wonder, Son-of-God, and the rest. I saw this freedom as the most precious possession I could acquire, and realized at the same time that in all likelihood I should never have it. Without being aware of it, I was no more than a sacrifice on the altar of Progress and Civilization. My youth was slipping away, and I was paying a terrible price for – well, for *what*? Having gone to school, at the decree of my all-powerful father? Having been chained to my books when most children of my age were out playing games? I did not exactly feel 'in love' with Eliza, but I certainy desired her. My desire was the kind most characteristic of the inexperienced male; I hardly dared admit it even to myself.

And now missing this meeting with her showed me in a vague yet compulsive fashion that if I went on as I was doing, against my natural bent, I should never be truly myself, or have any real individuality. I should never be anything but a point of view, a myth, a zero-like abstraction with which my fellow human beings could play at will, indifferent to my own desires or pleasures.

Soon Zambo got up and left, abandoning me to my unhappy dilemma, rather as though I were a drowning man being sucked under by the current, and beyond any hope of rescue. I was the most unlucky man in the world, I thought.

Apart from anything else, I was stifling. The room was far too hot and very small; the air was thick with smoke, and smelt of palm-wine, tobacco, and chewing-gum. I made a tremendous effort, which pushed me sluggishly, like a sack of coconuts, on to the platform of benevolent resignation and cordiality reserved for scapegoats such as myself. I no longer felt any desire to discourage the attentions of my audience; I abandoned my useless and egotistic attempts at revolt. I began to chew the local gum myself, and certainly nothing I could have done would have pleased them more.

'Look at him!' they exclaimed, audibly. 'Look, he's not snobbish, for all his learning. He's chewing gum *just like us*.'

At such moments, conscious of all those staring eyes converging on me like so many rays, I got the feeling that the atmospheric gravity had at least doubled its pressure. There was a hurricane-lamp burning on the table, its glass bulging and rounded like an old man's belly. The light it gave out was in fact not very strong, but to me it seemed as blinding as a searchlight set up at the same distance – at point-blank range, in fact. As a result they all saw me very clearly, and I could hardly make them out at all.

I sat there wondering to what extremes of idiocy the whole business could go. Lucky for me, I thought, that my friends couldn't see me pontificating in this half-witted fashion – and, anyway, what did it matter? I realized that my affection for these people outweighed any resentment I felt at my own ridiculous position. It was certainly a serious occasion as far as they were concerned.

'And what *do* the Whites teach you?' my hostess was still inquiring mercilessly.

'Oh – heaps of things —'

'Come on, then: tell us them.'

'Would you understand if I did?' I snapped. The remark was greeted with a murmur of disappointment. God, what a clanger, I thought. If I'm going to stay – and I must – I've got to behave myself.

'Listen to me, my boy,' said an old man, getting to his feet and interspersing his remarks with placatory gestures, as though he were soothing a baby. 'Listen: it doesn't matter if

64

we don't understand. Tell us all the same. For you the Whites are the real people, the people who matter, because you know their language. But we can't speak French, and we never went to school. For us *you* are the white man – you are the only person who can explain these mysteries to us. If you care for us at all, my son, do this thing for us. If you refuse, we've probably lost our only chance of ever being able to learn the white man's wisdom. Tell us, my son.'

He has a point there, I thought. These people were all so damnably persuasive.

'All right, then,' I said. 'They teach us – let's see – well, geography —'

'Geography?' exclaimed someone, fumbling over the unfamiliar syllables. 'What's that?'

I gave them what must have been the most feeble, certainly the most arguable definition of geography ever presented to any audience. I had never tried to formulate such a definition in my native tongue before, and now the thing had to be done for an audience who hung on my every word. Then, to make my ideas more intelligible, I decided to illustrate them with an example. I found myself (somewhat to my surprise) telling these simple people about New York – an inconceivable city to them, with its seven million inhabitants and skyscrapers of anything up to seventy-five floors, soaring up for a thousand feet. It was child's play to describe New York, probably because my only knowledge of it derived from the cinema. There was no longer any question of my drying up. I warmed to the theme, losing myself in an intoxicated sea of details. I imagined that my audience would be galvanized by the picture I conjured up; but, in fact, I went to all this trouble for nothing. (Still anxious to avoid giving them complexes, I omitted to tell them that Americans were in the habit of lynching Negroes in the street, simply because of the colour of their skin.) No; the really astonishing thing, which still bothers me in retrospect, was that America left these simple-minded people stone-cold indifferent.

I quickly changed the subject, just as the other evening the young guitarist had switched his rhythms; and without exactly knowing why, I played a Russian chord, to which they at once responded. (I probably acted on instinct; since I could spot at once what touched them or stirred them to enthusiasm. I must have been closer to them psychologically than I dreamed at the time.)

'Russia?' they asked. 'Where's that?'

'In the east, where the sun rises,' I said. 'The inhabitants are called Russians.'

I carefully avoided mentioning the more complicated aspects of Soviet farming (I had learnt a lot about the lecturer's art in one evening) and spread myself as fully as possible on the *kolkhoz* system. A *kolkhoz*, I declared, with an absolutely straight face, was a kind of field held in common, where every person worked for several days a week, spending the rest of his time on his own private allotment. After the harvest, the produce from the *kolkhoz* was distributed to each family according to their needs. At this point in my exposition the whole room exploded like a Brock's Benefit.

'Those sound like sensible people,' said one man, and another exclaimed how fond of one another they must be. 'A very pleasant country to live in,' observed a third, and others echoed him. I was astounded at the effect I was having. Full marks for this one, boy, I thought.

I decided to work this miraculous vein till it ran out. I waxed lyrical over tractors, and State farms, and the superb administration of rural communities. I pointed out what the system had achieved – production increased tenfold since the old days of individual, private cultivation. My audience positively panted with excitement. At one point I stopped to get my breath back – I had talked myself to a standstill: lecturing is by no means a sinecure – and a youngish man took advantage of my silence to comment on my previous remarks.

'These people are very like us at bottom,' he declared. 'They've got a sense of solidarity. They stand by one another, just as we do. Look at the way our women get through their work at ploughing-time – they all spend a day in one family's fields, and the next in another's, and so on. These people, what d'you call them, boy, eh? – oh yes, *Russians* – well, these Russians are extraordinarily like us. If only someone would give us some tractors – one to each tribe would do – we'd do just as good work, and perhaps produce ten times the amount we do now, as well. Only one tractor per tribe! But then who on earth would ever give *us* a tractor?'

Another man broke in, asking me if it was true that the *men* drove these tractors in the fields? He sounded a little worried. I told him yes, normally it was the men who did this type of work.

'What do the women do with their time, then?'

'They stay at home,' I said briskly. 'They stay at home to look after the children and manage the household generally. They do sometimes go out in the fields, but only to do light work. In Russia,' I added, seeing that the man was by no means resigned to this new scheme of existence, 'they consider that, since men are stronger than women, they ought to do the heavy labour; and personally I agree with them. Besides, Russian women are very pretty – they keep their looks right into middle age because they don't have to work so hard.'

I knew perfectly well that as my knowledge of real Russian life was very vague and sketchy, my only chance of coming through this ordeal unscathed was to invent my own version. The illusory nature of college learning could hardly have been better illustrated, as I learnt for myself that night. I was not without a certain pride in all I had learnt during the past academic year: yet at the first real test of my knowledge – a test imposed by genuine circumstance, not under the artificial conditions of an examination-room – I had already discovered vast gaps in the frontiers of my tiny kingdom. Now I was desperately trying to plug these gaps, and straining my imagination to the uttermost in the process. Yet if I had had to talk about Russia in my oral, I should have come out of it with flying colours – my oral, that is, not Russia.

Is there, as I am inclined to suspect, a kind of complicity, an unspoken agreement between even the severest examiner and any candidate? And if so, does this complicity not rest on the implied assumption (which the professor, at least, is consciously aware of) that all they both know is, in differing degrees, illusory and insubstantial? Pursuing this sour train of thought, I asked myself how many geography teachers in Western Europe and the areas under European influence, such as Central Africa, had any real or precise information about contemporary conditions in Russia? It was a depressing state of affairs if countless poor little bastards were forced to sacrifice their youth in assimilating a lot of fairy-tales.

My resentment against schools and educational systems mounted steadily as the days passed by. I saw a school as a kind of giant ogre, swallowing young boys, digesting them slowly, vomiting them up again sucked dry of all their youthful essence, mere skeletons.

Everything finally has to come to an end, and at last the party broke up.

My hostess thanked me for the evening's entertainment, and her husband promised to deliver a little present for me the following morning at my uncle's home.

As we walked back by ourselves my uncle said: 'They'll talk about you here for ages, boy.'

And I thought that this was the man who knew when to keep his mouth shut! He simply couldn't understand that I felt indifference – if not active distaste – at the thought of remaining a topic of interest here or anywhere else.

I lay awake for a while, intrigued by the sympathy and enthusiasm which my description of the Russian farming system had evoked in these local 'peasants'. And yet America had left them utterly indifferent. What was the reason for such differing reactions? Perhaps the economic, industrial, and material development of America contained some element of inhumanity, even monstrosity, which repelled these primitive country folk. Certainly Russia as I described it had a good deal more in common with their own way of life – as one of them had justly observed.

· · · ·

'Wake up,' I heard Zambo saying. 'Come on, little cousin! Open your eyes. You can go back to sleep later – if you want to. But just wake up for a moment —'

I seemed to be lying under water, with some great river slowly flowing by over my exhausted body. When I tried to open my eyes to see where I was, the water forced itself between my eyelids and stung the pupils. I was choking, ready to die. I tried to swim upwards to the surface, but I had no idea of how to swim and all my movements remained uncoordinated; so every time I made a little progress I sank back to the bottom almost at once. Yet in some mysterious way, slowly but certainly, I *was* emerging – my progress being steady enough for me to notice it and take fresh heart. Then, suddenly, my nose broke through to good clean air, and I breathed in deeply. It had been a narrow squeak.

'Are you awake yet?' Zambo was inquiring, persistently.

'Wha's marrer?' I grunted, still half asleep.

'Oh, do hurry up —'

'All right,' I said. 'There. Now I'm awake.'

'Not properly. Just one more effort, there's a good boy.'

'Look, I *am* awake,' I insisted. And then, suddenly, I was. There was a girl staring at me, with the kind of amused curiosity normally reserved for the inspection of new-born babies. (What's he like? Big or little? Good-looking or ugly? Noisy or peaceful?) My eyes obviously betrayed my astonishment, because Zambo at once said: 'All right; I can see you're awake this time. My word, you certainly are a sound sleeper!'

'That's not fair. You've no idea how late last night I got to bed.'

The girl smiled at this; her eyes seemed to me to reveal not so much passion as maternal affection.

'I'll leave you two now,' Zambo said. 'Father's working this morning, so you can talk as loud as you like – the old boy's busy with his furniture. You can have breakfast just when you like, they'll keep it hot for you. If anyone comes and knocks, say you're still in bed '

The girl kept staring at me, still half-smiling as though

69

secretly amused: it was how people often look when they watch a baby waking up. I must have seemed very bored; frantically I searched my mind for the right words and gestures. I sat up in bed to observe her better. She was not sitting with her back to the light, but sideways on, beside my bed, her face in profile. If I shifted about discreetly I could make a complete inventory of her charms. My God, how lovely she was! Her cheekbones stood out just far enough; her nose was small and pert, her mouth proud as well as sensual. Her whole personality breathed that air of calm, detached assurance which is only to be found in those girls who know what they want and can reflect on many past occasions when they got it: or so it seemed to me at the time. She was no country peasant; you could tell her a mile off as a real emancipated city-girl. She was entirely lacking in that submissive innocence which characterises a dutiful wife or daughter up-country.

She seemed to be waiting for something; but the longer I watched her, the less certain I became of just what it was. All women spend their lives waiting for something, I thought -- probably I'd read that somewhere – and they only differ in the degree of their foreknowledge. Some wait without really knowing what they're waiting for: those are the really innocent girls. The remainder know perfectly well.

Her easy carriage, her boldly encouraging expression, the almost over-ready smile, which seemed to say 'I know I've met you somewhere before' – all this increased her attractiveness for me. I *admired* her. But what I admired was still an abstraction, of course; I saw her as the embodiment of the Good-time Girl. In this respect we both suffered equally; other people treated us alike as abstract symbols. I was learning, she was Seductiveness. Unfortunately, while it was obvious that she liked clever boys, I wasn't attracted by experienced women. I wanted a virgin, a girl on the same footing as myself. And besides —

'How are you, Eliza?' I asked, stretching and yawning, in what I hoped was a casual voice.

'Fine, thank you. How did you know my name was Eliza?'

'My cousin told me.'

'Did he now? What a funny boy he is!'

I was beginning to detest her permanent, provocative half-smile, not to mention her air of expectation. For God's sake, what was she waiting for? (In fact, by this time I knew only too well.) For a moment I thought I would really achieve some positive action. I started to stretch out and take her by the hand, but the gesture lost all impetus half-way through, and my arm flopped back inertly on the bed once more. She looked at me with an air of astonishment and reproach, as though I had cheated her of something. I decided I ought to kiss her, but remained where I was, immovable. Oh Lord, I thought wildly, I must do *something*. But already I could imagine her contemptuous comment – 'My God, you can't be *that* young, it's just not possible!' I recalled my brother's diabolical remark: 'You've got to really satisfy her – and she must be a kindly woman. Otherwise —'

Could I really satisfy her? Or, to put it the other way, did she really love me? And, most important of all, was she kindly by nature? Even supposing she was, did her kindliness run to pity? 'My God, you can't be *that* young' – I could just hear her saying it. And that probably wouldn't be all she'd say; she might well ask sarcastically if I couldn't have spared her the trouble of coming in the first place. If I was to believe my brother (and his words were still uncomfortably fresh in my memory), some girls were nasty enough to ask a lover who failed to make the grade if *that* was all they could manage. 'A huge hulking fellow like you,' they'd say, 'you ought to be ashamed of yourself.'

I judged, by looking at her, that she was taller than I was. As we stared into each other's eyes, unable to break away, I felt a wave of cold indifference surge through me. I was filled with impotent resignation. Suddenly every muscle in my body relaxed; for all immediate and practical purposes I had become completely useless. I was not so much dismayed, however, as relieved; I had been afraid that my natural urges might push me into some complicated indiscretion against my

71

own better judgement. But for all this I felt a vague regret, somewhat akin to nostalgia, at not having taken this convenient opportunity – though I was at the same time congratulating myself on the prospect of not having to try again in future.

Eliza had turned away now, tired of smiling at me without effect, and visibly disconcerted. But all I thought was, Why, she's a head taller than I am, at the very least.

'What's your name?' she asked at length.

'Medza. Jean-Marie Medza. But you knew that perfectly well before you asked me.'

'I had been told, but I'd forgotten.'

She moved closer to me, and bent down as though to whisper in my ear. She gave off a strange odour, which was certainly artificial; she smelt as though she had put on the faintest dab of perfume. At that period all country folk, and even people like my family who lived near a country town, were absolutely convinced that the only reason a woman ever puts on scent is to cover up a nasty smell. The nasty smell, they reckoned, could only be caused by some unpleasant disease; and that, to us, meant some kind of V.D., which was the most unpleasant disease we knew. The realization that Eliza was probably wearing perfume had the effect (if such a thing was still possible) of making me even more frigid than before.

We remained a long time without speaking. It's a horrible thing when you simply can't think of one single remark to make to someone. We were close to one another merely in the sense that a couple of arm-chairs can be so described; but there was no binding link between us, no emotional unity.

Finally I managed to say: 'How did you get in here?'

'Your cousin brought me. We didn't have any difficulty.'

'They kept me up late last night,' I said.

'I know.'

Nothing but commonplace banalities, I thought.

The window was ajar, and through it I could see the grey dawn light coming up. When it became plain that we could stay there for years, Eliza waiting and me too nervous to move, she got up to go. There was an inscrutable expression on her face.

'Will you come back again?' I asked, hoping she wouldn't.

Without turning round she said she didn't know. No, I thought, studying her back view, she really is far too tall for me.

As soon as she had gone I got up and had a quick meal. Then I went down to the workshop, looking for my cousin, but no one was there but my uncle.

'Ah,' he said, 'I was hoping to have a word with you.'

He explained briefly and in an off-hand way (rather like a husband telling his wife what time he wants breakfast the following morning before setting out on a journey) that we were going out again that evening. A very respectable, worthy man had asked it as a particular favour. It did not seem to occur to my uncle that I might have any objection to such an arrangement.

Then he changed the subject. 'Have you see the present that arrived for you this morning?' he asked. He led me over to the window, and I looked in the direction that he pointed. Two young rams, the finest I had ever seen in my life, were standing there, cropping away at the grass, tethered to an orange-tree. They both were white-fleeced, with identical black saddles: they must have been twins. My uncle explained that this was the present my host of the previous night had promised me. I was touched by the gesture, but couldn't help wondering what I was to do with the wretched creatures.

I found my cousin in the cocoa-plantation. He was wielding his machete in a bored way and making more noise then progress. He straightened up when he saw me and grinned maliciously.

'Well?' he demanded, with some eagerness.

'Well what?'

'Oh, come on, tell. Don't be beastly. Tell me quick —'

'Tell you what, old chap?'

'How did it go? What's she like?'

'Well,' I said, 'she's certainly pretty. You were quite right about that —'

'No, no, what's she liked stripped off? And does she do it nicely? Let's have the details, h'm?'

'Sorry, I can't tell you.'

'Why not? You're not going to be a spoilsport, are you?'

'No, I'm no spoilsport; I can't tell you for a very good reason – I haven't see her naked.'

'Have you gone dotty?'

I said I hadn't.

'Well, what happened, then?'

I hummed and hawed.

'Come on, I want an explanation,' Zambo said.

'Nothing happened.'

'Nothing? What d'you mean? Didn't you like her?'

'No.'

'What? You *didn't*? Impossible!'

'That's right; I didn't.'

'But she's attractive enough —'

'Oh, she's attractive all right; but – if you see what I mean – she seems to have had a good deal of *experience*.'

He stared at me, eyes popping, as though I had suddenly turned into a gibbering imbecile. I tried to make my point a little clearer.

'That kind of woman's, well, dangerous, you know. You never know what you might pick up from them. There's a frightful risk.'

Conveniently, I remembered the words of warning and advice which my mother showered on me at the end of every holiday.

'What's dangerous about it?' inquired my cousin, still un-enlightened. Clearly *his* mother had taken very little care of his health, whether moral or physical.

I hesitated, wondering how to tackle the subject, and, in-deed, how to serve up my slanderous assertation: I had to avoid a direct accusation, and yet make it sound really serious. My cousin must suppose my hesitation due to the gravity

74

of what I had to reveal. I decided to make a generalized approach.

'Have you never heard of certain – ah – illnesses? Syphilis, gonorrhoea —'

'But what makes you think that? What reason have you to suppose —'

'I don't know, I just got that impression. She *uses scent*, you know.'

Zambo stared at the ground for a moment as if in thought. Then he raised his head, smiling and reassured.

'Look,' he said, 'I wouldn't mind at all if that was true; she's a proud bitch, and none of us have been good enough for her. Unfortunately it isn't.'

'Are you sure?'

'Certain. This isn't the city, you know. All the women here go and bathe in the river – you've seen the place. They always go together, and they bathe naked. Men go and hide in the bushes to watch them sometimes. They couldn't hide anything like that. Eliza bathes with the rest. If she hid herself, or refused to go in the water, there might be some grounds for suspicion. She doesn't. She behaves just like the rest, and no one's ever noticed anything unusual about her. Well?'

'What I don't understand is why she won't have anything to do with the rest of you.'

'You're not the only one to suppose it was because of some disease, but that isn't so. If Eliza was sick, everyone in the village would know about it. No, it's quite simple: we're not good enough for her. We're just not to her fancy, and that's that.'

'Why do you want me to go the limit with her?'

'I don't especially; she practically demanded to have you. I told you that before.'

It was all very convincing. Nevertheless, I was pretty sure he had aimed at revenging himself in a small way, if only at second-hand, for his own rejection. Why else should he have shown such eager interest in Eliza's naked charms, or her disposition in bed, and all the rest of it?

'Zambo,' I said heartily, 'women demand hard, unremitting work before they surrender. Keep on at her, don't be discouraged. You'll get what you want in the end, believe you me.'

'Do you think so?' He sounded at once incredulous and excited.

'I shouldn't have said so if I didn't. But as far as I'm concerned, in future you can count Eliza out. Oh, she's pretty enough, one of the best-looking girls I've ever seen in my life, I'll grant you that. But I don't know, when she's near me I just don't feel that way at all.'

'Would you like some other girl?'

'I was thinking about that,' I said, untruthfully. 'What I really want is a nice young girl who doesn't know her way about at all, if you get me. As long as she's young, sweet, and innocent, I don't care a damn about her looks. I'm sick to death of experienced old bags.'

Then, remembering my brother's words, I set about passing myself off as a case-hardened lecher. Before an admiring audience of one I embroidered my basic point. 'I've had enough of tarts who'll cut you a slice down any back alley, and that's all that was going back in the city. It gets tedious after a while, and I'm through with it.'

It looked as though he really believed me. Where I had the advantage over him was that over and beyond his stubbornness and his complexes, he had little imagination and no critical faculty whatsoever. I am firmly convinced today that as far as he was concerned I could have spent the rest of my life rejecting women on one excuse or another, and he would never have suspected my motives, let alone understood them.

Having produced this little fiction, I breathed a sigh of relief: once again I had won myself a reprieve.

Still, I told myself, I've got to have a woman some day; I can't stay a virgin for the rest of my life. Perhaps Eliza wouldn't have been quite so cutting after all. I was already beginning to regret my decision over Eliza, and wonder if I should ever get quite so good an opportunity again. A few hours ago I had

76

been as scared of her as the one survivor of a shipwreck faced with the prospect of making another voyage. Now I was developing a nostalgic yearning for her presence. But supposing Zambo actually dug out some innocent young girl for me? In that case, I decided, I would fall back on Eliza, take my courage in both hands, and *act*. I would even get some hints from my cousin, though that would mean admitting the unbelievable truth to him. I couldn't possible leave Kala in the same innocent condition as I arrived there.

Later that afternoon Zambo went off, as he put it, to 'go hunting' for me. He said he probably wouldn't see me again till about midnight. He was going to investigate the possibilities of the local Chief's family. This Chief was a polygamous old satyr with large numbers of daughters, some of them certainly very young. Zambo had heard a rumour that the Chief might come along this evening and listen to me talking. This would be to our advantage, especially if the elder members of his family came with him. This would give Zambo the chance to get into his house, wander round at his leisure, and make overtures to the girls. At least, that was what he said before he left me.

My host that evening was one of the village elders, an aged patriarch who lay on a bamboo litter, close to the red glow of the fire. The 'audience' was larger and more varied, with a larger proportion of young people, women, and children. The previous evening my listeners had mostly been men of mature age, who had enlivened the occasion by actively participating in debate. I was not so afraid of this happening on the second occasion, and had in any case prepared some set replies to what I guessed would be the inevitable questions.

The village Chief had actually condescended to appear in person, with an impressive entourage of attendants, and several of his wives. Just like the good old days, I thought. Besides, Zambo's predictions had been fulfilled. For a moment I let my mind dwell on my cousin. Fondly I pictured him wandering round the Chief's home, an indefatigable ghost, drawing various young girls aside on some flimsy pretext, and making his proposal to them with that exquisite self-assurance which never deserted him, even in unknown territory.

The crowd was swelling to vast proportions, and those who had failed to squeeze into the hut were now packed ten deep outside the door. There was a brief consultation as to how the proceedings were to begin. Since there were now far more people outside than in, it was suggested, why not hold the meeting in the courtyard?

Accordingly they carried the few chairs available outside. To judge by his expression, my host was obviously loath to abandon the fire, which seemed indispensable to his comfort; but here the individual will was subordinated to that of the group in a way which would have made even Lévy-Bruhl blink.

They all crowded round me, sitting on cane chairs or old wooden stools. Some squatted on their haunches, others remained standing, or leant against the wall to get a better view of me. I was sitting at a table, and to begin with they put a pressure-lamp in front of me to light me up a bit, a very modern affair. But soon it was plain that the hissing noise it made would completely drown my voice. I wasn't too clear at the best of times, and my nervousness had made me even more inaudible than usual. They took it away and brought out an ordinary old-fashioned hurricane-lamp instead. This had one great advantage: it made less noise than a sick child, and its light, instead of that white inhuman glare, shed a gentle yellowish glow on the scene. The effect was rather that of a sunny day as seen by someone suffering acutely from jaundice. I noticed that my uncle was seated at the table too, almost opposite me, as if to emphasize (I suppose) that the guest of honour was *his* nephew.

There were two heaped plates on the table in front of me, one containing gum, and the other bananas. They had obviously noticed me chewing gum the night before; but where they got the idea of the bananas from I can't imagine. Bananas always make me feel as if I'm choking when I eat them. I loathe bananas. All the same, I had to eat nearly a dozen that evening to please my hosts; they were all watching me eagerly. Over the chewing-gum I draw a veil; suffice it to say that I reached a point where I couldn't even taste its sharp tang any more, and that later the stuff robbed me of the sleep which I desperately needed and which I had more than earned.

How can I recall all the subjects which, on their insistence, I had to broach? I remember that one man – I'm not sure who, but I suspect it may have been that unspeakable person Endongolo – asked me an incredibly embarrassing question. He tried to make me explain a point which I had never let myself think about, the very idea of which terrified me: my future, and that of all my generation.

'Brother,' said this man (he was quite young, to judge by his mode of address), 'tell me, brother, what kind of job will you get when you finish your studies? And, to put it more widely, what sort of work will all you young college folk do after you leave?'

Yes indeed: what *would* I do when I finished my studies? And where did those studies themselves lead? We dreamed of all kinds of careers – medicine, academic research, the law, all the rest of it; but did we really believe in the possibility of such things?

I had really only applied myself to my studies at all because my father was ambitious on my behalf. He wanted me to get more and more diplomas and certificates, without bothering his head overmuch as to where they would get me. In short, I had been made to go to school, and then arranged things as best I could to suit myself: I had turned the whole thing into a game, something to pass the time away and amuse me.

It took no more than a couple of seconds for these notions to pass through my mind.

'Oh, we shall go into the various professions,' I said, without any great air of conviction. 'We shall teach in schools similar to mine —'

'Even if there are white children among the pupils?'

'Certainly.'

The man slapped the palms of both hands together as though to signify his astonishment.

'And what else will you do?' he inquired.

He was in the shadows, and I could not see him properly. I wanted to know what his face looked like – whether it reflected the sadistic torture he was inflicting on me. I was at the end of my tether; I wanted to yell for mercy, to throw in the sponge, anything.

'Heavens,' I stammered in my embarrassment, 'we shall administer justice – and work in offices – oh, we shall do a whole heap of things —'

Then the old Chief himself joined in.

'You won't be Chiefs then, such as I am?' he asked.

Apparently, to judge from what I was told later, the old man was trying to find out, in his tortuous way, if there was any cause for him to worry about such an eventuality.

'Oh no,' I replied thoughtlessly, without giving the idea much consideration.

The Chief seemed cut to the quick by my words. As though I had tried to belittle his office, he demanded aggressively: 'Why not, then? Why not? What's the matter with being a Chief?'

'Sir,' I said, half-laughing, 'chieftaincy is a hereditary function. You can't learn to be a Chief at school.'

'Ah, good,' he said, reassured. 'That's what I wanted to know.'

Everyone had suddenly gone very quiet. My uncle explained to me afterwards that they were waiting for me to put the old boy through the hoops a bit, that it was just what they hoped might happen. The Chief wasn't particularly popular in the village: people didn't like his excessive readiness to grease up the colonial administrators. In the days of the forced-labour gangs, he had been an energetic and zealous collaborator, requisitioning men, cattle, and goods with implacable fierceness. These levies were, indeed, demanded by the higher authorities, but on a somewhat smaller scale than he practised them.

He was not of a very great age, but he had run to bloated fat. What was being discussed that evening had no especial interest for him; nevertheless, he had made a point of coming, not in the interests of Security (which would have been understandable), but, it seemed, because he objected on principle to any public meeting, however unimportant, taking place in his territory without his being there in person. He was an odd character, as I found out later to my cost. But I must not get ahead of myself.

The next speaker, as far as I can remember, was a woman. Frowning with the effort of concentration, she said: 'When you get the kind of job you've mentioned, will you make plenty of money? You will, won't you?'

This is the evening for surprises, all right, I thought. On the assumption that this meeting would be just like its predecessor, I had worked out some very bright definitions of this and that. But once again life had caught me on the wrong foot: every question took me completely by surprise.

'I honestly don't know whether we shall make much money or not,' I replied, and that was no less than the truth.

Several people took this up. 'What a stupid question,' they said. 'Of course they'll make a lot. You don't think that after all those years at college they'll let themselves be treated dirt-cheap, do you?'

'Like we are,' added another.

The woman waited patiently till the hubbub died away; she had an idea, and she was sticking to it. A dark shadow suddenly loomed up in the lamplight: Zambo. He leaned over the table, very leisurely, and took a lump of gum. His father asked him, stiffly, whether he couldn't get some elsewhere.

'For heaven's sake, uncle,' I protested, 'what do you think I'm going to do with all that stuff? I couldn't get through it in a year.'

'It doesn't make any difference, my boy,' he replied in his calm, persuasive voice. 'You can always have *some* of it.'

Zambo's main object had been to bring his return to my attention; I guessed that he had done some good work – or perhaps I should say, work of which he was proud. This thought worried me slightly.

'Young man,' said the woman with the frown, when things had quietened down again, 'if you make all that money, that means you'll live like the white men, doesn't it?'

'How do you work that out?'

'You'll live in houses with a garden all round them, and a hedge to fence them off from each other. You'll sit about in the evening smoking cigarettes and reading newspapers. You'll drink your water from a tap, not fetch it from the spring. You'll lose your taste for palm-wine, and take to their red stuff instead. You'll travel around in a car, and have a tablecloth at dinner, and boys to wait on you. You'll speak nothing but *their* language. And perhaps, like them, you'll come to detest the sound of tom-toms in the night. Very well. But here's my real question – where do *we* come in to all this? Shall we be able to set foot in your houses as freely as we do in those of our own children? Will we be free to talk and enjoy ourselves there just as we like? Walk in with bare feet, as we're used to doing? Eat from the same dish as you do, even if we don't know how to use a fork? Will we be able to do all this?'

'Yes, of course you will,' I said, to deal with this point as briefly as possible. 'You'll be able to mix as freely with us as you would with your own family.'

'You really believe that?' she said, with infinite scepticism in her tone.

She had good cause for her scepticism.

I suddenly realized that I felt thirsty. I think it was my uncle that I mentioned the fact to. The information circulated in whispers from ear to ear till it finally reached my host. His wife at once went into the house and came out with a glass, which she polished energetically in the light of the hurricane-lamp.

'Is is clean enough now?' she asked.

'Of course,' I said, slightly irritated.

Then she went in search of a water-jar, but before she could pour the first drop into the glass, a chorus of protests arose among those present. Was this water clean and wholesome enough for me? Wasn't there a risk I might be made ill? It was no good my reassuring them; they stuck to their guns manfully.

'Wait, wait!' a young man suddenly shouted. He ran off quickly and came back a moment later brandishing a bottle, which he set down on the table with an air of triumph. My uncle uncorked the bottle and poured me out a drink. I was astonished, to begin with, by the smell of this brew. I put the glass to my lips, and then took it away again rapidly: the liquid was some kind of extremely powerful alcohol. Still, I was very thirsty, and they wouldn't let me drink water, so I had no choice in the matter. I drank the stuff in tiny sips, as much as I could of it; I should have emptied the glass if it had had a less unpleasant taste. Then I looked at the label on the bottle and realized that what I had been imbibing was neat American whisky. (I found out later that an American missionary in the area gave them a bottle of whisky occasionally in return for services rendered.)

No one had noticed that clouds were slowly piling up above the roofs of the village, and that the night was steadily becoming darker and more impenetrable.

From that day forward – indeed, from that very moment – two convictions have rooted themselves in my mind and refused to budge: first, that nothing in the whole world has a more horrible taste than American whisky, and second, that there's nothing like alcohol for putting you at your ease in any surroundings. Suddenly I felt happy and relaxed, full of exaggerated optimism and benevolence. The first dram of whisky I swallowed made me so confident and voluble that I finished off the glass. I had no doubt at the time that I was setting out along a strange route for an equally strange destination.

Now my explanatory remarks were loaded with all manner of convincing details: I found myself reassuring my audience, even flattering them. I told them comic anecdotes, and even invented a few of my own off the cuff. I don't know if any of them realized what had happened. All that mattered at the time was that my gusto pleased and amused them.

Then, suddenly, it began to rain. I have knocked about the world a good deal since then, but I remain convinced that nowhere except in my country are there to be found such violent, torrential cloud-bursts: they resemble a kind of divine barrage fired off by God against mankind. This was, in fact, one of those downpours which cut you off in mid-sentence and leave you standing, wherever you are, indoors or outside. The party broke up on the spot: my audience dispersed like a cloud of flies. My uncle grabbed me by one hand, as one would with a shoplifter caught in the act, or a child who has just had a hair's breadth escape from being run over. He took me home and then left me to my own devices. When I went into my room I found my cousin there waiting for me. He had lit the lamp and was lying stretched out on my bed. He got up suddenly when he saw me. He was beaming with pleasure because the rain had forced the old fogies to let me go sooner than they had intended. While I was undressing, my uncle poked his head round the door and said, holding a familiar object out to me: 'Here, boy, you forgot your bottle.'

He was quite right. I had, I was grateful to my uncle for bringing it back. I quickly hid it away, afraid that Zambo might claim his share of it.

'I've been to the Chief's place,' said my cousin, speaking almost in a whisper.

'Well?'

'It's going to be all right.'

'When? Tonight?'

The alcohol in my bloodstream was arousing me in other ways, too. I felt at that moment that, even with Eliza, I would have acquitted myself with a completely professional expertise.

'I've seen the young girls,' my cousin went on, baldly.

'We must be sure they're not *too* young,' I said, 'if you get me.'

'Of course, of course: don't worry, cousin, I know my way about. The girls are willing enough. Obviously they can't say

84

yes straight away, but I've got them sized up: they'll be only too delighted.'

He looked thoughtful for a moment. 'The difficult part,' he said reflectively, 'is getting them to come here.'

'Why?'

'Oh, you know perfectly well – their parents, my father —'

'In that case —'

'Listen, cousin, there's nothing doing tonight. Tomorrow perhaps. We'll see. We must work out a plan of campaign and stick to it in every detail.'

We sat on together for a little while longer; then he got up, clapped me on the shoulder and said: 'Good night, and don't be too impatient. One day soon everything'll come about just as we want it to.'

On this he left me. When I was alone I could not get to sleep for a while. I thrashed about in my bed, for no apparent reason. I decided the sheets were tickling me; it was as though they were covered with minute sharp points. I cocked an ear to my door, listening for every sound just as though I were expecting a visitor. I began to dream about Eliza: I pictured her stretched out naked beside me, my property for the whole night. I could do as I pleased with her in my dream, touch her wherever the fancy took me —

The invitations and evening parties succeeded each other endlessly. I was no longer my own master; more and more I had become my uncle's property. He farmed me out to the hosts who proposed themselves in my absence: every invitation was accepted, and when I reappeared he contented himself with informing me, very blandly, where our next visit was to be. I never once thought of protesting. You, who will remember my anarchic misdemeanours during that academic year, may well ask what was the cause of this astonishing passivity. I simply don't know the answer. All the same I can't help feeling that anyone, confronted with a man as self-confident and inscrutable as my uncle, would think twice about asserting themselves.

The morning after every visit valuable presents would arrive at my uncle's house: they were nearly always some kind of sheep. Soon it was no longer possible to tether them at random behind the house; we had to construct a sort of corral to park them in. I noticed (without any annoyance) that my uncle would often lean out of his workshop window and gaze at these yearlings with obvious affection.

As the size of the flock increased, so did his marks of respect and friendship towards me. He now went so far as to talk at great length to me, even to laugh in my company. This behaviour I found extremely flattering: my own father had never treated me as a friend, but rather as a kind of small dog, which you must avoid beating too often if you want to get the best out of it – and keep it tame. In my uncle's company, on the other hand, I felt very much a grown man, despite this habit he had of pushing me around from party to party: our friendship was perfectly genuine. In fact, the realization of my importance and irreplaceable uniqueness now began to colour my outlook more and more deeply. I became dangerously full of myself. I was, in short, developing a swelled head.

One morning, for want of anything better to do, I went down to the workshop to watch my uncle. Cabinet-making is a craft that exercises no particular fascination over me; on the other hand it involves certain gestures and repetitive actions which I find aesthetically satisfying, in an odd way, and which I never tire of watching. My uncle greeted me as I came in, though I forget the exact cheerful phrase he used. Then he paused for a longish interval, as though to mark off this interchange of courtesies from the lesson in higher philosophy which he was about to administer to me.

'My boy,' he said at length, still planing away at a long board while he talked, 'my boy, do you know what *blood* means?'

'*Blood*, uncle?'

'Yes. Blood.'

'Why, yes – er, that is, *yes*, I do know what it is —'

He lifted his plane from the wood, and looked directly at me.

His expression was a queer mixture of irony, curiosity, and exaggerated benevolence. It is an expression that may often be observed on the face of a bloody-minded examiner who has just asked a candidate a really fiendish question in the devout hope that he won't be able to answer it.

'Of course I know what blood is, uncle. It's not a difficult thing to define. Blood is a red liquid circulating through our veins and —'

He interrupted me with a loud bark of laughter; after which he shook his head a little, and returned to his planing. I was left open-mouthed with astonishment. His strokes with the plane were long, slow, and sure: it almost seemed as though he used the tool in this way because he knew I admired it so. He was stripped to the waist, and all his muscles seemed to form part of a single unified mechanism, that directed energy from its source in his body to the tips of the fingers which held the plane.

I watched him with a mixture of surprise, curiosity, and resentment. Surprise, because after asking me about the nature of blood he laughed in my face when I tried to answer him. Curiosity, because I would have given a good deal to know what *he* thought about blood. Resentment, because I was certain that my definition was sound – or would have been if he had let me finish it. Till this moment I had imagined myself a modest and reasonable person, not liable to be puffed up by my learning, such as it was – even though it had made a personality of me in Kala. But now the mildest joke at my expense had been enough to stir immediate resentment in me. What ridiculous creatures we are, when all's said and done!

After several minutes' work with the plane (oh, those calm, majestic strokes!) my uncle straightened up and addressed me once more.

'I said blood, true enough. But that wasn't exactly the kind of blood I had in mind.'

He paused for a moment, considering.

'Well, if you like, it's the same stuff, but I was thinking of it in a different way, a way that comes naturally to folk like our selves, who haven't been to school.'

He bent over his plane once more, and ran it several times up and down the board before going on.

'Do you know what kinship is?' he said at last. But before I had time to reply, he answered the question himself: 'Kinship means *blood-relationship.*'

'Ah, yes, now I understand —'

'It means that from the moment our kinship is established, the same blood flows in our veins. Or put it the other way round: the moment the same blood flows in our veins, we are bound by ties of kinship.'

He stopped again. His eyes never met mine. He brought out his words slowly, with apparent indifference. I lost the thread of the argument occasionally; he was perpetually wandering off into some corner or other of the workshop, still talking, to fetch a tool or some similar object. Soon I was compelled to walk behind him, pursuing him from corner to corner so as not to lose any of these impassioned revelations.

'That's a most important point,' he declared, in a sudden access of prolixity. 'The same blood runs in both our veins, boy. Think of that.'

After developing this theme at wearisome length (a characteristic trick over any idea that he took really seriously), he asked me whether this was a thing that the Whites taught me.

'What, uncle?' I asked.

'The importance of blood-relationship, of course.'

'No, uncle; they don't.'

'*No?*'

'No.'

He made no immediate comment on this, but returned to his work for some minutes. Then he stood up again and set about the exposition of this new theme. Did I realize how wrong the Whites were in not teaching us the importance of blood-relationship? It really must worry him, this problem, I thought. He must think it obsolutely vital.

He asked me several other questions, all bearing on the theme of blood-relationship.

'My boy,' he said, 'when you set out for Kala, you at once assumed, did you not, that you would stay with me and no one else?'

'Yes, uncle, of course I did.'

'Well, *why* did you assume that?'

'Because —'

I stopped short; I had been on the point of saying that it was old Bikokolo who had put the idea into my head. But now that I was taking a part in the game myself, I had developed a nose for a trap. This made me pull up just in time to avoid making such a *gaffe*.

'Come on, boy: tell me why.'

'Oh, I don't know – I've forgotten —'

'You've *forgotten*? But the explanation's perfectly simple – it's because we're blood-relations, of course.'

He stooped down to his work again, his face twisted into a kind of despairing grimace. It was just such an expression as is common among classics masters in the provinces, indicating that their pupils are incurably third-rate and will never be any use at anything, let alone classics. Then he stood up once more, with an air of conscientious determination. *Nil desperandum* was written all over him.

'When you're an important official in the city,' he said, 'where will I stay when I come to town?'

'With me, of course. Where else?'

'Why with you?'

'The obligations of blood-kinship —' I began.

'Ah! You've got the idea at last. I knew you'd understand.'

Everything, in his eyes, led back eventually to blood-kinship. For him it represented the keystone of all science, the ultimate word in every mystery, the foundation of his universal theory, his Euclidean hypothesis, his Fourth Dimension. Others might have invented relativity, the Quantum theory, and heaven knows what besides; but he had discovered, in blood-kinship, a whole unique cosmogony, irreplaceable, undeniable.

Now he was whistling tunelessly, one eye on the improvised sheep-pen outside.

'And what do you propose to do with your new property, eh?' he inquired. 'That flock of sheep, I mean. Have you any – er – *plans* for them?'

Well, well, well, I thought. This new theory of family obligations I've adopted is going to land me in some very expensive altruism all round, if I'm not mistaken.

'That's easily settled, uncle,' I said. 'I'll leave the sheep here for you.'

From one point of view I was highly relieved to get rid of the creatures with so little trouble. At least they wouldn't fall into my father's hands – an event which would merely have provided him with a fresh excuse for his endless speculations. But at my words my uncle burst out laughing once more.

'You'll leave me the lot, eh?'

'That's right, uncle.'

'No, no, no, my boy. It's very kind of you, but I couldn't accept that. Half the flock will be quite enough, quite enough. You can take the rest home with you, eh?'

Q.E.D., I thought. Proposition satisfactorily demonstrated. Couldn't the old boy have got to the point a bit earlier?

Having won game, set, and match, my uncle suddenly lapsed into sentimental reminiscence. His new mood was so unlike his normal behaviour that I began to wonder if he hadn't gone quietly off his head. He was staying with my father the day I was born, he told me; he couldn't remember exactly what took him there. It was a beautiful sunny day, apparently. My uncle saw me as a new-born baby: a lovely bonny child, he kept saying. When he set eyes on me he felt an indescribable joy. Now he knew the reason for this sensation.

I only listened to this farrago with half an ear. My uncle's personality defeated me completely. (The bland serenity of his convictions has always presented me with a kind of challenge.) But I refrained from pricking his bubble on this occasion; although in ways he was uncomfortably like my father, at least

I owed him a debt of gratitude for befriending me – even if his main object was my exploitation.

I was virtually confined to the village. I felt in the absurd position of an army corps waiting for a battle which the General Staff on both sides have completely forgotten about. No D-Day had been arranged. I couldn't go off for a ride on my bicycle. I seldom got the chance to go bathing with the boys; but these infrequent expeditions were great fun, and I was always delighted to see Duckfoot Johnny, Petrus Son-of-God, and Abraham the Boneless Wonder – all of whom, incidentally, were among Zambo's best friends, too.

The village laid siege to me socially from the early morning onwards. First of all there were the young boys. They invaded my uncle's house loaded with books and slates. They begged me to teach them to read, write, do sums, and understand the pictures in their books. Then came the grown men, who all wanted me to write letters for them. Since my arrival they had all taken it into their heads to place orders with European-style shops. I became their public scribe, scribbling away from morning to night under the absorbed and tireless gaze of an ever-increasing crowd.

Finally, there was the weaker sex – so weak, in fact, that I never found out just why young girls and women verging on middle age came and stared at me whenever they could manage it. They did nothing else, just stared: it was a simple kind of self-indulgence.

The evening parties, on the other hand, gradually lost their earlier attraction. Through hearing me talk so often, and asking me so many questions, the old folk became well enough informed about the subjects nearest their hearts for the edge to be taken off their inquisitiveness. Nevertheless, despite their gradual decline, these parties still took place every evening, like some inevitable ritual ceremony. It looked as though they would never stop till every head of every family in the village had had the honour of entertaining me. And looking back today I'm quite sure that even if I had, for whatever reason, prolonged my stay in Kala beyond the point where I had visited every house, there would still have been invitations pouring in. I should never have been left in peace.

Niam's wife, the original cause of my mission, had still not returned to the village. Every second day Zambo and I would go and call on her father. He was the only man in the place whose attitude to me fell somewhat short of benevolence; though it is very hard to make out just what he had against me personally. Zambo had finally, with his father's consent, taken over all responsibility for the affair. Therefore, it was he who now conducted discussions with Niam's father-in-law.

Several times, in an inexplicable access of zeal, Zambo provoked a quarrel; but it was never bad enough, luckily, to spread beyond the confines of that smoke-laden hut. I have a horror of scandal. I remember that one day he referred to Niam's wife, in the presence of her father, in terms that made her sound little better than a plain whore. At the time I felt, privately, that my cousin was laying it on a little thick. Later I found out that Zambo spoke no less than the exact truth.

I treated my bottle of whisky with great circumspection, rather like a woman with whom one anticipates a long affair and does not, therefore, want to explore too exhaustively in the first few nights. This attitude was due to the unlikelihood of anyone else offering me another bottle of so precious a fluid during my stay. I thought of this whisky as a source, providentially acquired, of all those qualities which I lacked by nature or which were liable to vanish in awkward predicaments – especially when dealing with my fellow men: spontaneous and cordial cheerfulness, volubility, the capacity to produce smart, instantaneous retorts, and take a strong, masterful line with women. The main reason why I husbanded my whisky so carefully was this. If Zambo brought me another experienced woman, I wanted to give myself a little Dutch courage. I had no intention of repeating my previous fiasco.

Unfortunately, through his very eagerness to oblige his young cousin, Zambo found more obstacles in his way than ever before. The girls were ready and willing enough, he told me; the difficult problem was to get them to my room. Day after day all his plans were spiked by one accident or another, and this irritated him horribly. From my own point of view, the prospect of being confronted with a girl no longer scared me so much. In the first place, I would be dealing with a girl who was, like myself, a virgin. In the second, I was relying on my bottle to see me through, much as a big-game hunter relies on his rifle when brought face to face with a gorilla.

One day, for his own peace of mind, Zambo arranged a little adventure without even notifying me in advance. That night, hours after I had dropped off to sleep, he came and woke me up again.

'Put on a loin-cloth,' he whispered, 'and follow me.'

My heart began to beat violently. I was as nervous as a partisan about to raid a strongly held enemy position. Before leaving I swallowed a stiff dose of whisky, which burnt my throat and stomach.

We crept along behind the houses, on tiptoe, taking every precaution, like burglars or any other law-breaker. I followed so close on my cousin's heels that I trod exactly in his footsteps – or as near as I could, anyway, since it was a dark night and I could hardly see a yard in front of me. After about twenty minutes, which seemed more like twenty centuries as far as I was concerned, we stopped outside one of the women's huts.

'Stay there. Don't move,' Zambo whispered.

I wondered where he was off to by himself. He skirted round the wall of the house behind which I was keeping watch, and came out on to the wide street which divided the village in two. Then he walked back a little way in the direction of my uncle's house, whistling a popular tune. He was still whistling when he passed out of earshot – or, to be more exact, that was the impression he managed to give. Only a minute or so after his whistling had died away he was back beside me once more. I felt him breathing in the darkness.

'She'll be here soon,' he said.

'Who?' I asked, nervously.

'Wait and see. She's very pretty and as young as they come – just how you wanted it.'

It was a cool night; a fresh breeze was ruffling the big leaves of the banana-trees. I shivered: after all, I had nothing on but a thin loin-cloth. But this unpleasant sensation only affected the lower half of my body. Above that I was amply warmed by the whisky, which was comfortingly prompt in its effects.

We did not have long to wait. A door creaked open discreetly, and my cousin gripped my arm in triumph.

'That's her,' he whispered.

Having no sure knowledge as to who 'she' might be, I felt far from completely at my ease.

A small shadowy figure appeared in silhouette at the corner of the house, crouching hesitantly like a young hare. It moved in our direction with exaggerated caution, but finally made up its mind to approach us. Zambo and the girl greeted each other and went into a whispering huddle. I was excluded from their deliberations, which lasted a long while and were characterized, to be quite honest, by a certain enjoyable liveliness. They were actually having an argument. Zambo wanted the girl to come to our house, just like that; but she claimed that her mother would be out looking for her if she wasn't back by a certain time. Then Zambo, apparently somewhat abashed – almost, I would have said, with a flea in his ear – came and whispered in my ear: 'All right; I'm off now. I won't be far away.'

Here goes, I thought. Zambo vanished in the darkness, and the girl still stood there in front of me. We were alone together. My throat was so dry that I felt as though I were in an oven, and I had to swallow my saliva to moisten it. I came closer to her. She said nothing, and would not look at me. She too was shivering, or pretending to shiver. I clasped her hand, and at once she moved towards me. Perhaps this was the gesture she had been waiting for. *Women are always waiting for something*, I thought.

I felt her breath flutter warmly against my chin. Then I held her close and kissed her on the mouth. It was a long kiss. When it was over she broke away nervously, as though she hadn't

94

particularly liked the way my breath smelt. Then I remembered that I must be reeking of whisky. But somehow, a moment later, I don't know how, she was pressing against me, and I gathered her in my arms, her body tight against mine for all its length, and we clasped one another in a chaste embrace that led nowhere. But what encouraged me was that she let me do it. She was wearing nothing but a thin sarong, and I could feel every contour of her young, well-muscled peasant's body.

Unable to control myself any longer, I pulled back her sarong with a clumsy, over-violent gesture, disproportionate to the act it was intended to facilitate. I uncovered all her secret places – breasts, belly, rounded thighs. Her body radiated a queer, intense, humid heat, exactly like the heat given off by the jungle when rain is followed by sunshine. She even smelt the same, the musty odour I always associate with jungle plants.

I let my hands wander all over her body. She made only the sketchiest gestures of protest; she was more concerned with keeping her sarong from slipping off and getting dirty on the damp ground. My God, what a girl she was! She burned like a torch. And how good she smelt! I cannot even begin to describe the exact quality of that smell. I only know that I've never found it again since, and I'm ageing so fast that now I probably never will.

Now I could feel the pressure of her body at every point of mine; and at the same time I felt worried by my own, inevitable, physical reactions. I was violently excited, but I didn't want her to notice this. Without knowing why, I was afraid she might be angry or shocked: I was the helpless victim of my own virgin scruples. It was the first time I had been in such close contact with any woman. I did nothing except hold her close to me, panting, and touch her where I wanted.

It may seem that all this must have taken some while. Not a bit of it. I was under this delusion myself at the time; but a delusion it was, as I found out afterwards when my cousin asked me why I had come back so quickly. He thought someone must have caught us at it.

The girl may have been exhausted by my horseplay, or, more probably, was unwilling to surrender herself in such uncomfortable conditions. Perhaps, too, she wanted our love-making to develop by slow degrees, as young girls tend to do, and not reach its climax at once and in so clumsy a fashion. Anyway, she broke away with a violent gesture, leaving me panting with half-satisfied desire. I went after her again and grabbed her by the arms. But this time she didn't come back for more; she said: 'No, don't – I'm scared – I mustn't be late, my mother's in that hut there. She heard me go out – she may get worried and come to see what's going on —'

'Let's shift our ground a bit, then,' I said.

'But I tell you my mother'll get suspicious if I stay out too long —'

We tugged and pulled in opposite directions, she trying to struggle free, while I wanted to keep her close to me, to recapture that moment of voluptuous ecstasy which I had just experienced, but which now seemed to be ebbing away with no hope of return.

'You don't want to go somewhere with me, then?' I asked.

'No, I'm afraid. It's not my fault, my mother's always around. Your cousin wanted me to do it with you, too. But it just isn't possible.'

She let me give her another long kiss on the lips, to please me, and then pulled slowly away from me. I made no further effort to restrain her.

'Well?' I asked.

'Well what?'

'When shall I see you again?'

'I don't know,' she said.

'Don't you *really*?'

'We'll have to wait for an opportunity – I can't tell in advance.'

'What's your name?'

'Edima. My name's Edima. If I ever get a moment free, I'll warn your cousin. When are you leaving?'

'I don't know. I can't tell in advance, either. Perhaps to-

96

morrow, even. It all depends on this woman I've come in search of. *I* don't know when she'll choose to turn up.'

'Won't you ever come back again after that?'

'How can I tell?'

She stood in thought for a moment, then made up her mind; at least, that was how it appeared to me.

'I must go now,' she said. 'We'll see what we can arrange. Good night.'

I went back to where my cousin was waiting. He was fuming at the thought of these wretched girls who all funked it at the last moment.

'I'll find one in the end who isn't afraid,' he said. 'She'll come all right.'

'Don't bother,' I said, 'please don't bother to look any farther. This one suits me very well indeed.'

Oh, the appalling sentimentality of adolescence! I didn't know a thing about this girl; I had hardly seen her face in the darkness; yet I was already thinking of her as an indispensable part of my existence. I was flooded with joy merely because I had embraced her for a few moments.

I lay awake for a long time that night, torn between two opposing sentiments. On the one hand I was amazed at the great discovery I had made, and delighted by its possibilities; but in the other hand I reproached myself bitterly for not having been more daring. Truth to tell, the mere touch of that warm, electric body had given me very real pleasure. At bottom, if I reproached myself for not having pushed matters farther, it was simply because this would, as I supposed, have increased the amount of pleasure I derived from the act. This was a theoretical notion which I afterwards modified: experience has convinced me of this cardinal truth – that the height of pleasure one can reach with a woman stops just short of intercourse itself. This may not be your opinion, but it represents my own sincere belief. I also contend that the best way to stay in love with a woman is never to go to bed with her. As long as you haven't slept with a girl you can still love her; but from the moment she opens her legs for you, she needs to be an angel, like Edima, or a saint to keep your affections.

I saw Edima again the following day, and realized then that I had, in fact, seen her several times before, though only at a distance. She was a wonderful girl, was Edima. She often passed by my uncle's house, and every time she kept an eye out for me eagerly. On this particular morning there were lots of small children playing about the house. Edima came in, and at first sat shyly in one corner. After a bit she came over to me, but still looked anxiously from time to time in the direction of the workshop: she was scared of my uncle. This was the day on which we became real friends. But because of the other people about the place, it was impossible for us to talk as we would have liked to do. Still, Edima pounced on every excuse – a dropped pencil, a casual joke, anything at all, in fact – to play with me and enjoy a good laugh as long as I shared it.

She was still the merest adolescent, a budding child. She must have been about fifteen; her body had developed precociously. She wore a dress of surprisingly simple cut. But how lovely she was! Her face, as yet totally unmarked by the lines and stresses of experience, made one think of a young child, a baby almost. But her body was a triumph of nature. Slim, rounded arms, delicately curving legs, a small high bosom, trim, plump, provocative buttocks – all these gave a simultaneous impression of firmness and fragility, like those healthy forest saplings she so resembled. Her hair was cropped close to her skull, which made her look somewhat like a young boy; but the similarity was contradicted by the sweet delicacy of her neck and jaw-line, the quicksilver subtlety of her expression, the shapeliness and beauty of her forehead. Most of the time she seemed to be smiling; and she did, in fact, find almost everything amusing.

That evening she came round again on the excuse that we were playing the gramophone. Eliza was there, too, silent, reproachful, in a really devilish temper; but this didn't stop Edima and me from enjoying ourselves under Zambo's delighted eyes. He found the situation highly piquant. Edima was like a favourite younger sister to me, and I felt a twinge of shame at beginning my amatory career with so innocent a girl. But she was not in the least bit afraid of me; on the contrary, it was I who at times felt nervous when confronted by a girl who embodied at once such strong elements of childishness and adult femininity.

I had been at Kala a fortnight now, and Niam's wife had still not returned from her little trip. The parties went on, night after night.

Then, abruptly, my stay at Kala entered a new phase; and here is how the great change took place.

When two men disputed the honour of entertaining me on any particular day, my uncle gave priority to the elder. This seemed only fair to me; I was still naïve enough to consider that the respect due to any person was in direct proportion to his age. Surely, I thought, that was obvious. Today I can see things more in perspective; and I can tell you without a shadow of doubt that my uncle wasn't nearly so disinterested in his motives as I was. Let me explain.

In general, a man's fortune – this word must be understood in its widest sense – was, in Kala, conditioned by his age. An old man was in a better position than a young one to give away a few head of cattle, thanks to a system which in the spheres of economics, law, and tradition alike was designed by old men, to benefit old men. As a result, an old man could always give more substantial presents than a young one. Besides this, there was the matrimonial system to be considered: this too was biased in favour of age, so that a young man had less chance of getting *married* than his elders. As a result, in Kala a woman is an infallible sign of male prosperity, equivalent to a good refrigerator and automobile in America. And, just as in America, it's not enough for a Babbitt to be a successful businessman or have a substantial sum in the bank. He must prove the fact by showing off his fridge and his Chrysler; if he doesn't, people look down on him. In the same way, it was essential to be married in Kala if you wanted public esteem.

My uncle, who was not only a social conformer of the most abject kind, but also tended to look well ahead, thus always gave preference to older claimants. There were an extraordinary number of old people living in Kala.

To look at the problem from a different angle for a moment, Kala was, as I think I have already said, a really enormous village. It was quite clear to me that if I stayed on for a whole year the old folk would still be monopolizing me, while their juniors would be getting resentful and frustrated. That, in fact, was exactly what happened. The younger generation felt all the more annoyed since the bone of contention – me, that is – was one of themselves, a boy of their own age. What it came to, more or less, was the feeling that they were being deprived of their natural rights.

This, at all events, was what Endongolo gave me to understand.

Endongolo was a big youth, rather boorish and uncouth in his manner. He had come to nearly all the evening meetings, and asked a number of questions pertinent enough to make me take some notice of him. There was a certain rough charm about his expression, and he spoke with a modesty that was sincere, if a little overdone. He felt obliged to laugh at the least hint of a joke, and generally behaved with relentless and overwhelming amiability. He would have been a saint of sorts if it hadn't been for a powerful weakness where palm-wine was concerned – or, indeed, any liquor that could make you forget the miseries of this world, if only for a few brief hours. It was no surprise to find that he was perpetually half-pickled: such unswerving good-humour would be humanly impossible on any other explanation. I was very fond of him, though he was well over thirty – as opposed to Duckfoot Johnny, Abraham the Boneless Wonder, Petrus Son-of-God, and Zambo, whose ages ranged from twenty to twenty-five. Endongolo was, in fact, of the intermediary generation between the old, properly speaking, and the young.

I had just finished breakfast that morning when in he came, a calabash slung from one shoulder by a cord.

'Good morning,' he said, smiling in a conspiratorial yet slightly obsequious fashion.

'Good morning, old fellow,' I said, as pleasantly as I could. At least I could try to earn a free drink of palm-wine.

We shook hands, with the firm grasp common among people who are planning to become associates in some grandiose scheme. Grinning with embarrassment, he remained standing till I begged him to take a seat. Now normally that never happened here; guests never waited for anyone to tell them to sit down, but got into the most comfortable chair within range without a second thought. It struck me at once that he must have something on his mind.

He was staring round the room as though it was his first visit to the house. He fingered the furniture, stared at every object with minute attention, made flattering compliments about the owner (who was away at the time) with the obvious intention of letting some of the lustre be reflected on me. While he talked, he was scratching his bare legs, and his nails left long whitish marks on them: clearly he hadn't had a bath that morning. I wondered in some amusement how many times in a month he did.

'Since this is your house,' he said presently, 'I wonder if you could find some glasses?'

I went and got them out of the cupboard. He poured wine into them both, and we tossed off the first glassful at one gulp. He promptly refilled them. He seemed in high good spirits, like a man who has just got married, or concluded a successful deal. We drained glass after glass without uttering a word, like two condemned criminals enjoying life for the last time before execution. I went on drinking because he filled my glass up so rapidly that he seemed to want me to drink the stuff equally fast. His own haste, I suspect, was due to his fear that some third party might turn up and insist on sharing the calabash with us.

A bunch of children poured into the house and descended on me, brandishing slates and shrieking in a deafening treble chorus. Endongolo let out a burst of pleased laughter, somewhat to my surprise. Then he said how sorry he was for these poor kids : they'd be miserable when I was gone. He went on and on about how well I'd taught them, and how efficient my methods were – the more intelligent ones had already made great progress, as he, Endongolo, could testify, even though illiterate himself. Then, without any warning, he suddenly switched subjects.

'I didn't go to work this morning,' he confided. 'No jungle chores for me!'

'No? Why not?' I asked, trying to simulate some interest in his affairs. 'You aren't ill, are you?'

He laughed. 'Ill? Heavens, no. Look, chum, some people get ill, some don't.'

'Oh, yes?'

'Too true. There are some people who never get ill. Like me, for instance,' he burst out laughing.

'What luck,' I said, politely.

'Isn't it, chum?' He laughed again, 'Look, it's this way – when I don't feel too good, see, I get hold of a full calabash of this stuff and scoff the lot. Half an hour later I'm all set to sing my head off, and the illness is out of the window —' He went into a long giggling paroxysm.

'That's hardly surprising.'

'It isn't, eh?' Laughter rendered him momentarily speechless. 'Tell you what I think – this good old palm-wine, it's what you might call my penicillin.'

At that time all the country folk took penicillin to be a universal panacea for every ill.

We laughed together, but I still hadn't gathered the reason for his visit. But after filling our glasses yet again, he began to come to the point.

'No,' he said, 'I didn't go to work this morning. Nor did my sister, either.'

'No?'

'Oh, you know my sister – she's the girl who —' and he launched into a long description. Though he assured me that I must have seen her on several occasions, the description conveyed nothing to me. Besides, I hardly heard what he was saying, being constantly engaged with the children who were milling round me, climbing on my knees, and pulling my ears and hair.

'Yes,' he resumed, 'my sister hasn't gone out to work today, either.' He gurgled with laughter. 'I'm very fond of my little sister. She's amusing. This morning, though, she wasn't at all pleased, oh no!'

'No?'

'No. You see, I took my decision last night, and carefully didn't warn her beforehand. It was only this morning that I told her we'd be staying at home all day. She was just going off to the fields with the other women. She's a hard-working girl, my little sister. She doesn't like to miss a day.'

'I can understand that.'

'That's right, isn't it?' He choked and spluttered. 'I like you, you know. Just as much as I like my sister. You're the kind that understands, first go off. Yes, I'm as fond of you as I am of my sister —'

He paused, and emptied his glass. Then he went on: 'Yes, my sister's always telling me that if we don't work no one's going to help us, that we're only poor orphans, we've got no family —'

'No one'll help you because you're orphans?'

'That's right – our parents are dead. My father went first. My sister was only a tiny baby at the time —'

He gave me a long, rambling account of his parents' death. When he had finished he paused, and put on an appropriately mournful expression. Then, suddenly, like a man waking up, he made a nervous gesture, a kind of flick of the fingers as though he were chasing away an intrusive fly. Then he made a valiant effort to recapture the thread of the conversation, and I wondered, somewhat amused, whether he'd be able to manage it after such a digression. Judge of my surprise, then, when after one of his incomprehensible bursts of laughter I heard him say: 'Yes, yes, my sister was in a fine paddy because she hates being made to lose a day's work. But when I explained everything to her, that changed everything, oh yes! She could hardly hold herself in for joy then —'

'When you explained *what*?'

'Why, that *you* were the reason for her missing a day's work. Oh, it was a different story then – one day more or less, what did it matter —'

'But how was it because of me?' I asked, bewildered, staring at him in some trepidation.

Endongolo blushed. He had the expression of a man about to ask a large favour which he has done nothing to deserve, but which he hopes to extract from you despite your knowing what he's up to.

'I'll tell you. Every one of us here in Kala is glad to have you with us. We all like you very much, and we'd all like to entertain you in our homes, even though we haven't got much to offer you. We'd still get a great deal of pleasure out of your company. Who can tell whether we'll ever see you again? It was pure chance that brought you here, pure chance that your path crossed ours. The trouble is, your uncle always gives priority to the old buffers, and they monopolize you every evening. There are a hell of a lot of old buffers in this place too.'

He paused, and poured out two more glassfuls. We drank, and he went on: 'Well, chum, I said to myself, "I might just as well take a day off and invite Jean-Marie home in working hours." After all, this isn't like a town job, and I'm not employed by the Whites. I work my own fields, I'm my own master, I can do as I please.' He roared with laughter.

After a pause he added: 'Well, boy, that's how it is. Would you care to come and spend an hour or two at my place today?'

'Today?'

'Too true; I've lost one day's work already, and I can't afford to lose another. Besides, I've made all the preparations in advance. See what I mean?'

He sat there, eyes popping, mouth agape, his whole attitude one of touching supplication. I thought: What a passion they all have for confronting you with a *fait accompli*.

'All right,' I said, rather nervously, 'I'll come.'

'Ah, capital, I knew you wouldn't refuse. I like you a lot, chum. Thanks a million.'

'What sort of time?' I asked.

'Oh, whenever you like. We've got all day to ourselves, you know. What about – oh, eleven o'clock, midday, something like that. All right?'

'Fine.'

'Thanks again,' he said, and poured the sticky, opaque dregs from the calabash into our glasses. We knocked it back just like the rest.

Then he went off, after a flowery and ceremonious leave-taking. I heard him whistling to celebrate his victory as he slouched off down the road. I wanted to laugh, but didn't. It wasn't really something to laugh at.

My cousin had gone off to work on the cocoa-plantation; but as he returned even earlier than usual that day, he accompanied me on my visit to Endongolo, who gave us both a warm welcome. The sister also appeared; she had charming manners, but was distinctly plain.

I have seldom enjoyed a better meal, or eaten with better appetite. The atmosphere was relaxed and friendly. I drank large quantities of palm-wine, which made me extremely cheerful and somewhat disinclined to listen to Endongolo's sad reminiscences. He was determined to tell me the story of his life, and despite appearances it had been anything but gay. It seems likely that Endongolo was occasionally liable to go maudlin-tipsy, which would explain everything. Some day soon, he told me, he intended to get married; but for the moment he lived with his dear little sister, who was just as good as a wife – 'in ways, that is – he, he, he! – only in ways!'

I had drunk enough to feel indifferent to his sufferings. I wondered, a trifle maliciously, what difference it would make to him when he *was* married.

Some people will tell you, naively, that wine makes you happy – a great mistake. Wine intoxicates: that is its essential property, or virtue, if you prefer it. It is the state of intoxication

which may have some moral influence on you, not the wine
per se. Yet intoxication does not, in fact, make you feel happy.
What it does do is insulate you from actuality. It is this state
of detachment which (according to the circumstances) ap-
pears to the drinker in the guise of benevolence or misfortune.
Surely, at its deepest level, such self-deception can bring nothing but misery? Can this indifference to reality, to the world
that the bulk of mankind inhabits, be anything but perverse
escapism?

Zambo sat there, untroubled by such thoughts, shovelling
great helpings of food into his mouth. He spoke seldom, and
when he did it was either a commonplace remark or an obscenity. The meal was drawing near its close when, from the
courtyard outside, there came the sound of a girl's voice, shrill
and imperious.

'Well, well,' Zambo said, with malicious pleasure, 'there's
Edima.'

'Are you sure it's her?' I asked, a little disconcerted.

'I'm quite sure it's her, dear cousin of mine. I'll go and fetch
her in. That'll make you grateful, won't it, eh?'

He strolled to the doorway and hailed Edima. She de-
murred at first, but presently came in, with three tiny children
trailing behind her. In fact, she must have seen us come past to
Endongolo's place and, either instinctively or deliberately –
who knows? – have followed, with the private intention of
somehow joining us. Since our first meeting, Edima had found
a good excuse for no longer helping her mother in the fields:
she now looked after her little brothers. Up till now they had
been in the care of a young boy who, told off to look after his
own brothers, had taken on Edima's as well. They seemed to
have got on pretty well this way; but Edima had found a
golden excuse to stay in the village, she had persuaded her
mother to agree, and the thing was done.

She was literally grey with dust; she must have spent all
morning rolling about on the ground with her brothers, like
the child she was. We invited her in to eat with us. She did
little more than nibble at her food, and spent all the time

glancing furtively in my direction, with private winks and grins that I had to pretend not to notice. It was obvious that she was delighted to be in my company.

When the meal was over, Edima came and perched on my knees, without being asked. I thought privately that she showed remarkable boldness, and admired her for it. I put my arms round her. Her muscles were firm and resilient; her buttocks, resting on my thighs, felt remarkably hard. Taking advantage of a moment when Zambo and Endongolo were arguing fiercely about something or other, she whispered in my ear: 'Will you leave soon?'

'I think so,' I said, teasingly.

'When?'

'I'm not sure. Why do you want to know?'

'Nothing. . . . Is it fun living in the city?'

'Not nearly such fun as being here. Oh, I see: you want me to take you to the city, is that it?'

She burst into a long paroxysm of laughter. I was pleased to have found (as it seemed) the way to tickle her sense of humour. It was, without doubt, to the palm-wine that I owed my astounding form.

Endongolo's sister, on the other hand, was studying me with a minute attention that was only equalled by her discreet modesty, the sort of attention only merited under normal conditions by visitors from another planet.

It was only when evening was obviously drawing in that Endongolo released his poor guests, though they had been pining for their liberty from the moment the meal was over. When I totted it up, I found that, willy-nilly, I had given up not two hours, but five to the wretched man. He was certainly right in one respect: our paths had crossed by accident.

Endongolo's scheme soon caught on and spread. Since the old folk monopolized me for the evening and a large part of the night, the younger generation began to take up my time during the day. This unforeseen turn of events wasn't at all to my uncle's liking. He would doubtless have preferred me to have devoted all my time to my elders, day and night alike, and it isn't hard to see why. But – probably for the first time in his life – events got ahead of him, and he gave up trying to influence them as he would have wished. He could still console himself with the evening parties, however, and, above all, with the knowledge that half the goods that accrued as a result of these sessions would revert to him.

For days on end I was to be seen dashing desperately round the village, up and down from house to house, with Zambo and Edima following. They made a striking pair: my handsome cousin, his torso muscled like a Greek demi-god, and the strange Edima, half-woman, half-child, whom I at once desired and cherished like a sister, and who, slowly but surely, was becoming the centre of my existence. My attitude towards her had now become that of God towards mankind; I could afford to wait. There was no hurry. So far an unfortunate combination of circumstances had fenced us in, depriving us of all chance of freedom, or any opportunity for intimacy. But I was sure that a loophole would soon appear.

During these rushed and hectic days, I really drained my cup to the dregs. I learnt just what degree of disgust and desperation can be produced by the necessity of day after day spending up to five hours with predictable people – men, that is, who after a certain amount of food and drink can be guaranteed to tell you the story – the miserable story, inevitably, of their life. It is extraordinary how different lives resemble one another, superficial details apart: they all seem to be miserable. I doubt if there is a single human being who could say, with a straight face, 'I've got everything out of life I wanted. I ask nothing more.'

On my way back from these visits, as I trudged the length of this endless village with Zambo and Edima in attendance, I had to run the gauntlet of the women. Most of them were back from the fields by now, and they stood in their doorways airing prophecies of marriage between me and Edima, hardly bothering to lower their voices. This I found both flattering and irksome. They all referred to Edima, with a nod and a wink, as 'the Chief's daughter', as though it was unthinkable that I could fall in love with anyone of lower station.

The children came scampering round us, with shrill cries, their numbers increasing at each house we passed. It was a dismal procession. I often wondered what my father would think if he could have seen me now.

Like the fabulous machine that wouldn't stop once it was put in motion, the evening parties continued, but with the difference that the young people (for their own good reasons) no longer attended them.

The flock of sheep was growing almost as we watched. It was the essential part of the proceedings as far as my uncle was concerned, and he showed a quite touching solicitude for the creatures. Presently there was added to the spoils a noisy poultry-yard: the young people who could afford to give me presents at all offered me chickens, which were the only livestock they possessed in any quantity. His own hen-run rapidly proving inadequate to house the newcomers, my uncle built another, in record time. We were becoming quite prosperous.

All the same, the most pleasant memory I have of Kala, apart from Edima, is the party four of my young friends gave me. They were already united by indissoluble ties of friendship and brotherhood, but this solemn occasion merely served to bind them more closely. (I would speak of their 'association' if this word did not seem out of place in dealing with a people entirely innocent of modern notions concerning economics and capitalism.)

The four were none other than Duckfoot Johnny, Abraham the Boneless Wonder, Petrus Son-of-God – to name them in descending order of age. It is without doubt because of the gratitude I owe them for this party that I remember not only their names, but the smallest details of their eccentric and colourful personalities. Oh, I forgot to mention the fourth – my cousin Zambo, as ever was. All the same, to be quite honest,

Zambo played a very small part in the organization and arrangement of these festivities. This was because he had to comply with the orders of an authoritarian, a positively tyrannical father, who made him take his machete every morning and go off to the cocoa-plantation, where he made an impressive noise for a while, and gave the general impression of working. We all know how much time can be wasted at *that* kind of game. Anyway, my handsome cousin didn't need to play a prominent part in the preparation of these memorable festivities in order to engrave his appearance and his name on my memory.

The four young men had planned on such a grandiose scale that their party had to be spread over several days in order to be fully appreciated. It was finally wound up four days after it began, in a welter of curses, broken pots, spilt wine, and general drunkenness; there may even have been some fighting, but that I'm not sure about, since I took myself off smartly towards the end for – to me – very cogent reasons of security. But I am getting ahead of my story.

Early one morning Duckfoot Johnny (or St John of Kala), Abraham the Boneless Wonder, and Petrus Son-of-God came round to the house and found me sitting on the veranda. They seemed somewhat excited, and were arguing in loud voices, so that a fair proportion of the village could hear them. Now, contrary to what both the Censor and Principal of my college had claimed during the whole of an academic year, I am a shy person (or was this merely due to different surroundings?) and I hate anything which attracts people's attention. I was therefore disposed to condemn my friends in advance. When they reached me, they took such a brusque tone in addressing me that I seemed confirmed in my judgement.

'Hey, chum,' they said, 'where the hell's your cousin got to?'

'I don't know for certain,' I replied, without much enthusiam. 'I suppose he'll be around soon. Would you care to wait for him?'

They ignored this, and each in turn pressed me to go off with them. 'Come on, Jean-Marie,' they said. 'Don't let yourself be tied up the whole time with old fogies and children. You haven't got any engagements today, so come with us instead.'

'Old men and kids,' said Duckfoot Johnny, reinforcing his remarks with extravagant gestures, 'old men and kids have a lot in common with the salamander. You know what a salamander's like? Once it's got its claws into anything it never lets go, horrible little sod of an animal. I'll tell you a story while I'm on the subject. One day I went out with my two lurchers, and we put up a salamander, a lovely juicy specimen, believe you me. I sent the dogs after it, and they were so hot on its tail that it tried to get away by climbing up the trunk of a baobab tree. Salamanders have a hard life, one way and another.

'The trouble was, it was too out of breath and exhausted to climb the tree fast enough; and there I was with my hunting-spear. Quicker than God's own lightning I am with a spear, no kidding. Well, what do you think I did? I nipped over to the tree, looked up, and saw my little chum the salamander still clambering up the trunk. I poised my spear, called on the spirit of my dead father to guide my arm, and nailed that salamander to the tree, fair and square. I watched it writhing about for a bit, and then had to quieten my dogs down – they were barking like mad; thought the salamander was going to get away. I waited till the little beast was good and dead, and then climbed the baobab tree myself. But I hadn't reckoned on its claws. Great long hooked things, like the claws they give Satan in church murals. It had driven them deep into the tree-trunk – so deep that I couldn't shift them, even though it was dead. I had to go down again and get my machete. It took me half the day to cut the bastard out.'

'Too true,' put in Petrus Son-of-God. 'You're a sensible fellow, Jean-Marie. I know what you're thinking. "If Duckfoot J. had called his friends to help him, Zambo, the Boneless Wonder, and old Son-of-God, he'd have got the salamander out in half the time and with a damn sight less trouble." Isn't that right? But look at it this way. If he'd roped us in, we'd known he'd caught a salamander, and that would have meant sharing it with us. He wasn't having *that*, oh no, not old Duckfoot, the greedy, guzzling bastard. He'd rather sweat it out on his own, so long as he kept his secret and didn't have to share his tit-bit with anyone else. You may not know it, but there's nothing quite so savoury as roast salamander. Isn't that the truth, Duckfoot, eh?'

'I can tell you something to beat that,' said the Boneless Wonder, who normally was a taciturn sort of person. 'This queer fellow' – he gestured at Duckfoot Johnny – 'once shut himself up alone for a whole week. We began to get a bit worried; what on earth had happened? Where had he got to? The truth of the matter was, he hadn't gone anywhere. He was gorging away at his bloody salamander. As he just said himself, it's not every day you catch one. Oh, the greedy beast!'

'My dear friends,' protested Duckfoot Johnny in a hurt voice, 'my *very* dear friends – I couldn't ask for your help on this particular occasion; you weren't around to be asked. I've always told you the truth, haven't I? That day you simply weren't there, and that was that.'

'All three of us?' said Zambo, sceptically. He had heard our voices and come over to join us.

'Yes: all three of you.'

'Look at him; just look at him,' said Zambo, in a pleasant parody of his father's tone and phraseology when roused to paternal wrath. 'Will you kindly tell us any occasion when the three of us have been away at once, even for a single day? I'm surprised that salamander didn't kill you with the belly-ache; you must have gorged it down at one go, like a boa-constrictor.'

'Christ Almighty!' exclaimed Duckfoot Johnny, a martyred expression on his face. 'They want to kill me off now, and all because of a wretched little salamander! I can't even remember what it tasted like, it was all so long ago. If I died you'd be sorry soon enough. Look. I've just laid a dozen or so traps on the far side of the river. With any luck we'll catch a fine antelope in a day or two. Be patient, my friends: I'll soon recompense you for this miserable salamander —' He suddenly broke off, grinning. 'And now I come to think of it,' he added, 'I never ate that salamander at all. Don't you remember? I sent it to that man whose daughter I wanted to marry. He demanded salamanders in exchange for his daughter; he *was* an old gourmet. I obviously didn't send him enough salamanders; if I had, I'd be married to his daughter now, wouldn't I?'

This incoherent and specious excuse amused us considerably.

'Anyway,' he went on, 'I was talking to Jean-Marie, not you. There you have it, dear boy; old folks and kids are just like salamanders. They get their claws into you even when they're dead. Now, unhook yourself just for today, pull out all the claws, and come along with us. You too, Zambo.'

This speech persuaded me – not that I needed much persuading. As for Zambo, he was all set for fun and games, anyway; he had not bothered his head about excuses. All the same, as he pointed out, he would have to take certain elementary precautions. 'It's on account of my old man,' he explained. 'But don't worry; I'll catch you up by a short-cut.'

'Don't tell me you're scared of your parents, with all those muscles!' said Son-of-God, sarcastically.

'It's all very well for you to talk; your father doesn't bother his head about you.'

'No; and why? Because I stood up to him till he stopped trying to order me around.'

Zambo said, in a worried voice: 'Which route are you going to take?'

'We're going to the baptismal fountain of St John of Kala,' Son-of-God announced, 'to the Living Spring itself. You know where that is?'

'Yes, I think so.'

Zambo went off, his long machete in one hand, ostensibly towards the cocoa-plantation. He took care to pass directly in front of the workshop where his father was busy.

'Of course he knows where my baptismal fountain is,' snorted Duckfoot Johnny. 'It'd be damn funny if he didn't. Where do you suppose he goes to slake that incurable thirst of his when the fit takes him? My poor little pots and jars; they're always running dry. Zambo, of course. I've never actually caught him red-handed yet, he's a sly devil. But it won't be long now. When I catch him I'll turn him over to you, Abraham. You taught little kids their catechism for a couple of years at – two hundred and fifty francs a month, wasn't it? You can improve his moral standards. Teach him the difference between *meum* and *tuum*. That might stop him sneaking in and stealing my wine.'

After walking for some way through the jungle, we came out in a narrow clearing, where four palm-trees lay sleeping peacefully side by side, like exhausted giants.

We sat down at a little distance from the four trunks, and Duckfoot Johnny detached from each the jar into which the sap had dripped and fermented. These jars he set down in front of us. Then he distributed rudimentary cups made out of split coconut shells, and announced his drinking rules.

'As some of us,' he observed sententiously, looking straight at Son-of-God, 'have permanently parched throats, all glasses will be refilled simultaneously. That way none of us will be caught short.'

I took my courage in both hands, realizing that I was fairly caught in a drinking contest. I wondered how long it would be before I had to admit defeat, and whether it wouldn't be better to do so straight away. But to keep my end up, I decided at least to string along on the first round. We helped ourselves by plunging our goblets into a full jar.

'Now don't forget,' said Duckfoot Johnny, still handing out instructions, 'the first four rounds must be drunk at one go – no heel-taps.'

'Why?' I inquired, in some alarm.

'*Why?* So that my house may always be blessed with plenty, of course. Don't you know *anything* in your part of the country?'

'I don't think we have that custom. I've never heard anyone mention it.'

All three of them burst out laughing. I felt very much on my own. Then, suddenly, Zambo appeared, a broad grin on his face. He sat down and grabbed a goblet.

On the sixth round I showed all the symptoms of exhaustion and incipient surrender. My cousin, observing this, told Duck-foot Johnny not to make me drink too much, as I wasn't used to it.

How grateful I was to him! Blood-kinship does have some meaning after all, I thought. My scepticism about my uncle's theories was severely shaken from that moment.

'He may not be used to it,' said Duckfoot Johnny, calmly re-filling my goblet without even consulting me, 'he may not be used to it *yet*, but he will be soon. And by the way, Zambo, how is it that you know the way to my Living Fountains all by yourself? Explain this mystery to me.'

'There's no mystery about it,' Zambo said, 'and you know that perfectly well. You brought me here yourself the first time.'

'Are you sure? Wasn't it a *different* Living Fountain I took you to then?'

'Are you insinuating,' Zambo said, 'that I pay visits to your liquor-caches when you aren't there?'

'I'm not insinuating anything, dear boy. I simply asked you a question.'

There followed a long and pointless argument. At the end of it we still weren't any wiser as to whether Duckfoot Johnny had or hadn't, taken Zambo for his first visit to the Living Foun-tains. The Boneless Wonder, anxious to clinch matters, an-nounced: 'Religion teaches us that —'

'Which religion?' Son-of-God demanded.

'Catholicism,' said the Boneless Wonder.

'Excellent. I'm quite willing to hear you expound Catholic-ism, so long as you tell us afterwards what the other religions have to say, too.'

'*Are* there any other religions?'

'Well, what about St John of Kala?'

'All right, all right,' said the Boneless Wonder. 'Let's begin with Catholicism, though. It teaches us two main principles:

firstly, that we shouldn't covet our neighbour's goods. That means we mustn't steal from him. Render unto Caesar the things which are Caesar's, and to God the things which are God's. Secondly: never judge any person rashly. Never accuse people, that is, without having formal proof of their guilt. That's all.'

'You're prejudiced, that's obvious,' said Duckfoot Johnny, with heavy irony. '*And* pickled. I've never been able to make out these little pansies who can't take a glass of wine without going off the deep end.' He suddenly turned on me. 'I gather you're not interested in Eliza?' he said. 'What's the matter? Don't you find her attractive? Or are you just scared of women?'

'It's merely a question of taste,' I said, with that self-confidence which seems an inevitable by-product of the initial stages of drunkenness.

'Merely a question of taste, I agree. But funny all the same. Very funny.'

'Why is it funny?' protested the Boneless Wonder. 'Why on earth should it be? If he doesn't want a girl, you can't bully him into having her. Besides, for my money he's done the right thing; he's paid her out in her own coin. Tit for tat. We ought be be pleased.'

'There's one thing which could have been arranged if anyone had thought of it,' said Son-of-God dreamily, 'Jean-Marie here could have made a private arrangement with me. He could have invited this girl in one night, and then left me to deal with her in bed. It'd have been pitch-dark; she wouldn't have known the difference. Christ, what a going-over I'd have given her! Lordy! They'd have had to take her to hospital the next day. I'm telling you.'

'She'd have known who it was straight off,' said Duckfoot Johnny, laughing; 'you stink like a garbage-heap.'

'Every *real* man stinks,' countered Son-of-God.

For some time now Zambo and I had operated a private sleight-of-hand manœuvre over the drinks. I would fill my own goblet and put it down beside him; he would replace it with the one he had just emptied. Right till the end of the party no one spotted this little dodge. I remained in perpetual astonishment as to how any normally constituted human being, with only one stomach, could possibly absorb such rivers of wine. There would obviously be no stopping them till the four jars were completely empty.

When we finally got up to go, only one of us walked unsteadily, and that (appropriately enough) was the Boneless Wonder. Duckfoot Johnny looked at him with a certain disdain.

'You ought to be ashamed of yourself,' he said. 'Look at the little city boy – he can hold his drink better than you can. See how straight he's walking!'

A tiny grin quirked round the corner of Zambo's mouth, like a flower-bud unfolding. Duckfoot Johnny seemed totally impervious to alcohol; the only unusual thing he did was to fling one arm round my shoulders and tell me that henceforth I would be his closest friend, because, despite my shocking upbringing, I drank better than any of them.

'The first time I saw you,' he said, 'I wasn't too sure about you. I know these city slickers; they're a different kind of chap from us altogether. You must be the exception that proves the rule. I propose to *adopt* you, Jean-Marie.'

His breath stank most unpleasantly, which detracted somewhat from his sentiments. Next he began to teach me a song. This song delighted me so much that I not only learnt it by heart, but later took the trouble to translate it. In this way I hoped to preserve it for those future generations who will probably never drink palm-wine in their lives, and will, as a result, be ignorant of the poetic genius which this divine liquor can inspire. Here is the song:

> When I get a scolding from some old nell
> I think of my poor dead mother,
> And I say to myself, Ah, what the hell?
> It's an awful life, dear mother –
> But honestly, what the hell?

When I hear some old sorcerer flogging his luck
I think of my poor dead father;
And I say to myself, What a load of muck!
It's an awful life, dear father –
But hell, what a load of muck!

When some old trollop bawls me out
I think of my poor dead mother;
And I say to myself, You stupid old trout!
It's an awful life, dear mother!
But hell, what a stupid old trout!

When some great bastard hands me the bull
I think of my poor dead father;
And I say to myself, Bull's only bull –
It's an awful life, dear father –
But remember, bull's only bull!

This song probably doesn't strike you as the kind of thing
liable to rouse a sophisticated reader to transports of enthusiasm. But, believe me, there's nothing like palm-wine for adding a special edge to your sophistication. I know. I've tried
it. If you aren't convinced, go away and top up on palm-
wine, read these verses over again, and tell me how you feel
about them when you have. Anyway, my translation probably
stinks.

Duckfoot Johnny made me go on singing this song till I got
it word-perfect, knew the tune by heart, and interpreted it with
enough vigour and emotion to satisfy him. It was no use my
telling him, in a perfectly friendly way, that in fact I hadn't
myself lost either of my parents. He answered my every protest
with the remark that I should lose them one day anyhow, and
then I'd be an orphan like everyone else – him, for example.
After that I gave up and set about rendering the song in a
weepy-sentimental vein, which delighted Duckfoot Johnny
enormously. For all these reasons I have given this song the
title of 'The Little Orphan's Lament'.

We crossed the river and went on walking for some time, the Boneless Wonder still swaying and staggering about, and Zambo still with that tiny secretive smile at one corner of his mouth. Son-of-God was making a prodigious effort to convince him that the best religion in the world remained that of St John of Kala, which consisted of two basic commandments: When you are thirsty, drink anything except water; and never forgo any occasion for making love, whatever time of day it may be (Sundays included).

Such was our state of mind when we finally emerged into open country – so-called. This particular year the 'fields' belonging to the village of Kala were nothing but one single vast clearing in the jungle. The men had simply burnt away all the forest undergrowth they could, and then divided the resultant land into individual or, more accurately, family allotments. This tract, therefore, was even bigger than Kala village itself.

The harvesting season was nearly over, and the air was heavy with the smell of roasted ground-nuts. The fields were suffused with a yellowish glow from the coarse stems and clustering leaves of the maize crop. The women were bent over the furrows, delicately hoeing up the last ground-nut plants, while young boys and girls gathered them and stripped off the ripe nuts. At more or less regular intervals a thin spiral of smoke wound its nervous way up to the sky, where boys were squatting round an improvised fire, roasting ground-nuts or maize-ears. There was a mingled scent of freshly-turned earth, ripe crops, and sprouting vegetables, while all around the jungle stood austerely on guard in the glory of its sombre greenery.

My friends quickly borrowed three baskets from the women, and began to trot about the field, saying to every girl they passed at work: 'Take pity on a poor beggar asking for charity. Give me a few ground-nuts. God will reward you one day for your generosity. Take pity on a poor unhappy soul. Give me a few ground-nuts!'

The women straightened up, giggling, and finally all

contributed a handful of ground-nuts; not a single one of them refused. The three baskets were soon filled. Then Duckfoot Johnny put his foot down.

'Greedy beggars,' he observed. 'It's not worth robbing them of any more of their ground-nuts; we've got more than enough already. On your way!'

We got back to the village in the middle of the afternoon, and they promptly began to shell the ground-nuts they had scrounged so cheaply.

The Boneless Wonder, who had sobered up a little, declared: 'You've got to admit it, we've our little city mascot to thank for this haul. If he hadn't been there, no one would have taken any notice of us at all.'

'That's why we invited him to come along,' Duckfoot Johnny answered imperturbably.

It was at this point in their preparations that I left them. I have only the haziest idea of what happened afterwards. As far as I can make out, they went off the next day and tried to sell their ground-nuts in a near-by market. The day after that, so I was told, they set about buying up some poultry and a sheep at bargain prices. They also started rounding up their girl-friends, without whom the party would have been a complete flop as far as they were concerned. As I have hinted already, it was the fourth day, no earlier, that marked their true apotheosis.

As it happened, this fourth day was a Sunday.

I had been warned early in the morning not to wander off anywhere, but to hold myself at the disposition of Duckfoot Johnny and his gang.

About eleven o'clock I was sought out by a delegation sent by Duckfoot Johnny, which consisted of the Boneless Wonder, Petrus Son-of-God, and three other young fellows whose names I have forgotten. I made my way through the village escorted by these toughs, rather like an American diplomat under the protection of his private eyes.

Duckfoot Johnny's hut had been done up in the most remarkable – and unusual – way for this party. To begin with, it had actually been swept: a highly rare occurrence. Next it had been decorated with garlands of mango-leaves and palm-branches. Those in charge of the festivities, not yet satisfied with their efforts, had adorned the walls, *faute de mieux*, with sacred pictures: on one side a Sacred Heart, on the other a Crucifixion, with the Immaculate Conception in the middle. There were a large number of people present, mostly young men and girls.

'Listen to me!' Duckfoot Johnny shouted, clapping his hands. 'There's only one guest here – our young friend from the city. Everything you see here – food, drink, the lot – has been prepared specially for him. As for the rest of you, I'm grateful to you for coming along to give our guest a good time, but mind you only eat and drink what you're given!'

It was a bit off-hand, to be sure, but it expressed what he wanted to get across clearly enough.

The next speaker was Zambo. 'Gentlemen of Kala —' he began.

'Kala for ever!' they shouted. 'Hurrah for Kala!'

'I suggest,' my cousin went on, 'that you do not bother about either eating or drinking tonight. Leave such vulgar urges to the riffraff from other villages round about, who are so ignorant of the first laws of hospitality that they don't even know how to entertain a guest! In my opinion, what we should do is dance – that's the only way to create the proper atmosphere for such an occasion.'

This lame speech was received with ecstatic bursts of applause. Then they all sang a kind of national anthem – at any rate, the word 'Kala' occurred in every verse. I can't remember any more about it than that; I have very little sympathy with nations as small as Kala, and even less with their patriotic anthems.

Then the party began. We were served by young Kala girls, although, from what I heard, it seemed that the actual cooking had been done by the boys' sweethearts, who came from other neighbouring tribes. Despite Zambo's exhortations and

Duckfoot Johnny's magisterial warning, the company managed to get plenty to eat and drink, never missing an opportunity of draining a glass or swallowing a tasty morsel. One single table had been set up in the middle of the hut, just for me. The rest ate off plates on the floor. The party had been going a long while before Zambo's 'atmosphere' was produced, and they began to dance the *assiko* in that voluptuous, contorted style so much more characteristic of Kala than any national anthem.

At this moment, when everyone's attention was distracted from me, I took advantage of the general excitement to beckon Edima over to me. She was gaily excited as always, and enjoying the occasion enormously. I made her sit on my knee; then I kissed her, once, and looked round to see if anyone was watching us. They weren't, so I kissed her again. And again. It went on for a long time, and now she was demanding to be kissed herself. It was all great fun, especially for me: I hadn't stopped drinking since the party started. I tried to make Edima join me, but she firmly refused to touch a drop.

Nothing happened to spoil this cheerful atmosphere till evening began to close in. Perhaps the young dancers got progressively more tired and irritated as they went on; there may even have been more concrete complaints, but anyway, the atmosphere suddenly cooled off. It all started with Son-of-God having a squabble with a big-mouthed boy who claimed to have been insulted. This squabble subsided after a moment or two and we thought no more about it. But a little later Big-Mouth began kicking the jars of palm-wine with considerable vigour; they (somewhat naturally) broke, and spilt their contents all over the floor. This rapidly turned into a kind of wonderful white lake, to the rage and despair of Duckfoot Johnny: after all, it was his hut. He hopped about from one foot to the other and ran out of saints to invoke in his moment of crisis. What decided my faithful cousin Zambo to take me away from this scene of potential murder was that, shortly after Big-Mouth started kicking jars and calabashes to bits, bottles began to be shied at the empty space where they had been. (That probably explains why they didn't hit anybody.)

It would be hard to explain exactly what lay behind this affair. Big-Mouth, apparently, belonged to a tribe in the neighbourhood of Kala, and thought that Son-of-God's remarks had been intended as a personal insult. He therefore decided to recompense himself for this insult by getting an inordinate amount of free food and drink. They gave him as much food as he wanted because the place was running over with it; but when it came to wine, they replied very politely that they were sorry, but they couldn't oblige him; even Living Fountains, they said, were liable to dry up. At this point, unconvinced by their arguments, he sailed into action.

You may perhaps wonder what this foreigner was doing on such an occasion among the young people of Kala. Let me explain. In Kala, when you sacrifice an animal (as it might be the sheep which Duckfoot Johnny and his friends had bought the day before this memorable occasion) you have to call in a man from an outside tribe to cut its throat – though he must also have connections with Kala on his mother's side. This seems to be a well-established tradition. Accordingly Duckfoot Johnny had called in Big-Mouth, who fulfilled all the necessary conditions. He had cut the beast's throat and afterwards quartered it. Duckfoot Johnny swore that he had been rewarded more than generously for his services, and this made his unspeakable action even harder to forgive.

I said earlier that I wasn't certain whether blows were actually exchanged; some people told me that in fact they were. Those officially responsible for the occasion, as it were – meaning Duckfoot Johnny, the Boneless Wonder, Son-of-God, and Zambo – merely informed me that Big-Mouth had been politely thrown out. You may wonder whether it is possible to throw someone out (even politely) without a certain amount of argument and strong-arm stuff; if so, your opinion coincides with my own, though heaven knows that doesn't mean much.

Anyway, I was peacefully asleep by the time these putative acts of violence were taking place, so I could cheerfully abjure all responsibility for them.

Such, in short, were the reasons why I retained so many ineradicable memories of this particular day.

CHAPTER THREE

In the course of which the reader will become convinced that the final climax of this story is at last in sight – a conviction which is, most unfortunately, mistaken.

IT was just as the fourth week of my stay at Kala was beginning that, suddenly and unexpectedly, things came to a head.

To begin with, there were the celebrations at the Chief's house.

As you may know, it isn't enough for a man simply to marry a woman in our country, even though he follows the prescribed ceremony out to the letter. There must also be a delegation of men and women from the young bride's village to escort her to her husband's house – an occasion (especially in Kala) for endless festivities.

The Chief had just married another wife – his seventh, as far as I can remember – and he had been in a fine state of anxiety for weeks, wondering what day his tribal in-laws would choose to deliver his bride on the doorstep. The tribe in question carefully concealed the day they had selected : they wanted to give the Chief a surprise. Warning of the event depends on how well off the bridegroom is. A man of slight means has to be notified in advance, so that he can make special preparations for these highly important days of celebration. What use was there, they argued, in notifying so substantial a man of property as the Chief? What extra preparations would *he* need to make? He had everything at his beck and call the whole time.

In fact the Chief, like most people who made a pointed display of their wealth, was by no means very well off. So much so, indeed, that it seemed he had been sending round to the elders in his fief, inviting them to make 'voluntary' contributions in kind and service when the great day arrived, and to hold themselves unreservedly at his disposal. What's more, he kept on at them relentlessly till they gave him a formal promise of assistance. His approach varied between two extremes: at one end of the scale came amiable blackmail, which invoked friendship, clan-brotherhood, honour, and those patriotic sentiments which demand that every decent citizen should support his sovereign if the latter is in danger of losing face to outsiders. At the other, he descended to pure intimidation, threatening sanctions of every kind against his wretched victim.

Yes, I know what you're going to say. How, after the revolutionary changes brought about by the new Constitution of October 1946, could any Chief still blackmail his constituents in this fashion? That's what you're wondering, isn't it? And I'll tell you why: you belong to the city, to urban society. So do I; and that was why I asked such questions myself at the time.

Let me explain, then. To begin with, even though the Chief's threats might have been mere bluff, they were still liable to be quite effective. His constituents, or, more accurately, his subjects, had little idea (if any) of the terms of the October 1946 Constitution. As a result they were hardly likely to invoke it; they remembered instead the very real powers which the old man had wielded till 1946: powers which he himself still pretended to hold.

In sober truth the Chief's threats – any Chief's threats – had very little bluff about them. With the help and advice of their administrative superiors – the colonial officers, that is – they had perfected a new system of oppression. This, while superficially conforming with the law's requirements, enabled them to keep the population absolutely under their thumb, and exploit them exactly as they wished. Their routine methods had a certain disarming precision. For example, there was a massive set of regulations in force up-country, which laid it down as a basic principle that forced-labour gangs were henceforward abolished. There remained on the books, however, one clause in minute print stating that the authorities had power to requisition labour in the event of a 'public emergency'. The definition of a 'public emergency' is liable to various interpretations; that of the colonial administration was conveniently elastic. It provoked disagreement, but retained a monopoly of execution.

One more instance: when any man wanted a certificate authorizing him to purchase a gun, or car, or sewing-machine, or anything on the restricted schedule, his Chief's approval was required before the certificate was granted. A simple but far-reaching measure. It will be seen, then, that the Chief's power was very real and no mere obsolete figure of speech.

Nevertheless, shortly before the delegation from his new bride's family was due to arrive, the Chief was still keyed up with anxiety, for all the formal promises of assistance he had (more or less honestly) extracted from his dependants. The fact of the matter was that, at the very heart of his tiny domain, a fierce opposition had ranged itself against him; an opposition all the more implacable for being composed of young people, who are, as an age-group, notoriously ruthless.

It was inevitable that, in Kala, the younger element should have undertaken the task of spiking the Chief's guns. Their opposition was anarchic enough, and largely consisted of windy threats; but, nevertheless, it got its results, after a fashion. As soon as the Chief had extorted a promise of aid, in kind or service, for the coming celebrations, several young men would pay a prompt visit to the unlucky victim, and explain to him at great length that the Chief no longer had any real authority. Therefore, they would conclude, he was not entitled to such feudal tributes.

In this way every victory the Chief won was in danger of being lost overnight by a rallying in force of the opposition. In point of fact, however, the rising generation gave their elders far too much trouble through sheer rowdyism to be able to convince them seriously on any scale. Furthermore, a few successes scored by the opposition did nothing to shake the Chief's basic power. No, the main function of the young was to create fear: they acted as a kind of bugbear.

News spreads in this country with enormous speed. The bride's tribal delegation was very much mistaken if it thought it could *really* take the Chief unawares when it came to the point.

On the Tuesday morning following the party thrown by Duckfoot Johnny and his gang, a rumour went round that the bridal delegation, having left two days before, was now encamped quite close to Kala. They would arrive, however leisurely their progress, that very day. Detailed accounts were passed on about the number of men in the delegation, how it was made up, the kind of presents being brought, the songs they were rehearsing to accompany their arrival in Kala, and all the rest of it.

In Kala itself the women stopped going out to do field-work and the men remained at home. Everyone wanted to be sure of seeing the new bride, who was unknown in the village.

The bridal delegation actually reached Kala in mid-afternoon, just when it was hottest. It consisted of a long procession, led by young country boys dressed in the most appalling taste. There followed a solid body of old gaffers, armed with fly-whisks and sticking their bellies out as they marched. They wore ceremonial loin-cloths that hung down nearly to their ankles, and their gait betrayed a carefully assumed dignity and self-confidence. They had carefully schooled their expressions in a premature appearance of gorged satisfaction, and you could see the *clichés* about friendship, eternal alliance, and the rest of it visibly forming on their lips. The procession was rounded off by a few rather bored rams, and some poultry in wicker baskets. The women of Kala gave a few very half-hearted cheers; it was too hot to work up any real enthusiasm.

It wasn't till the delegation had vanished into the Chief's house that people tumbled to the fact that they hadn't yet seen the new bride – or, at least, hadn't been able to distinguish her from the others.

'There was one woman had her head veiled in silk – d'you suppose that was the one?' someone suggested.

'No, no, no. *I* think it was the one in that gauzy dress with the funny pattern on it – all those little men paddling canoes, you know —'

'Nonsense,' broke in another woman, 'that girl was far too young.'

'Well, the bride's supposed to be almost a child, isn't she?'

'Possibly, but not below the age of puberty, surely?'

'Ah, well, we'll find out this evening.'

This was true enough; the presentation of the new bride took place, traditionally, only after darkness had fallen. The Chief had been polite – or politic – enough to invite me to this ceremony. He had even thrown the invitation open to my uncle as well, though this turned out to be a superfluous gesture: the old boy assumed he was coming, anyway. After much argument I persuaded Zambo to accompany us as well.

The tom-toms and xylophones were banging away in the courtyard outside the Chief's house when we got there, like a heard of stampeding elephants: they positively made the ground tremble. Round about the drummers and musicians a number of young girls were dancing in wild abandon, under the fatherly eye of a bright full moon. They were clapping their hands like mad, as though the syncopated thunder of drums and xylophones weren't enough for them. It was a hellish din: a steady rumbling roar that occasionally burst into peals of thunder, the vibrant, protracted note of a great waterfall plunging into the abyss. Through this uproar there could be heard from time to time the thin, clear sound of women chanting. It was a hopeless, derisory sort of effort; it made me think of a butterfly sitting on the broad leaf of a mangrove-tree while a tropical storm is coming down. Or perhaps a little girl caught up in a riot.

The three of us, my uncle, Zambo and I, skirted the court-yard where the dancing was going on, and went slowly up the main steps that led to the Chief's reception-room. At our entry the Chief rose with some eagerness and came to meet us, as though we had been ambassadors of some major foreign power at his court, and worthy of every mark of honour and prece-dence. On this notable occasion he seemed, as it were, almost transfigured into handsomeness; somehow he looked less grossly fat, and his face less puffy than usual. Certainly his Chief's court dress, with its epaulettes and rows of decorations, did give him a certain air of distinction. Tall and broad-shouldered, he stood there looking like a somewhat ageing Apollo. But his language remained as coarse and violent as ever, in sharp contrast to his imposing presence – and much to his guests' disappointment.

Everybody fell silent when they saw us arrive. The Chief took me round the entire room and made me shake hands with everyone present; this took an unconscionable time, as there were crowds of guests. Then he conducted all three of us to the best arm-chairs in the room, and we seated ourselves. An occasional table was set before us, on which stood a most im-pressive array of bottles: palm-wine, red wine. American whisky, rum, brandy, and heaven knows what else. At first I drank very moderately, keeping one eye out for Edima among the girls who were waiting on us. But though I stared round the room till my eyes practically popped out of my head, there wasn't a sign of her. What on earth had happened to the girl? I hadn't seen her for two days – in fact, since Duckfoot Johnny's party, which ended – as far as I was concerned – in the strategic withdrawal I have already related.

Zambo sat beside me, in a gay and confident mood which seemed, however, to have little to do with the spectacle con-fronting us. He was, to judge by appearances, lost in a kind of cheerful brown study; while my uncle, too, remained wrapped up in mysterious thoughts of his own. It wasn't hard to see that everybody was whispering to each other about me, but I paid very little attention: I was far too concerned with wondering what had become of Edima. Outside, that diabolic, frenzied drumming went on without an instant's pause.

After a little, since I couldn't solve the problem presented by Edima's mysterious absence, I began to drink more and more heavily – a common consequence of such a situation.

Suddenly there was a really frightful outburst of noise, like two dozen trains steaming out of a station at once, or every siren in a city wailing into the void simultaneously. Nobody in the reception-room seemed particularly put out by this racket, but I must have jumped with fright, because I remember my cousin stifling a laugh, pinching my arm, and saying: 'Don't be scared, cousin – there's nothing to be afraid of. They're just bringing the old bastard's little bit of frippet in, that's all. Just you wait: we're going to have some fun.'

The thunder of the drums and xylophones redoubled in volume and intensity; it nearly cracked my eardrums. A procession of women was coming up the steps, slowly, very dignified, and simultaneously emitting the most piercing yoo-hoos, like demented yodellers. In the middle of them walked a girl of about the same age as Edima, who seemed highly astonished and disconcerted by the whole proceedings – almost, indeed, ashamed. The women marched into the reception-room, still howling away like mad. They were followed by the drummers and musicians, still playing at full blast. At one point I really thought I was going to burst into fragments under the pressure of this tremendous din. The young girls who had, a few minutes before, been dancing nicely *au clair de lune*, now burst in as well, bobbing their tits at us like nobody's business.

At last silence fell: the leader of the delegation got up, took the Chief's young wife by the hand, and made a leisurely recital of her pedigree and the more distinguished feats of arms achieved by her ancestors. This included all honours won during the period of German colonization. He then went on, his voice throbbing with emotion, to say how much, how very much, this notably happy marriage they were celebrating to-day meant to the members of his own tribe. Finally he wound up with the words: 'Chief, I now give your wife into your hands.'

He spoke more literally than he knew. The Chief promptly seized hold of the girl, as though she were a parcel just delivered and, with some ceremony, settled her into an armchair. He performed this operation with enough delicacy to prevent the spectacle of such an old pig with a young girl in his arms being wholly offensive – even to me.

The band began to play again, and the women set up an even louder yelping and screeching than before. The girls started clapping their hands in time to the music, and everybody nodded their heads sagely as though they'd just heard a news bulletin announcing some national victory. The girls formed a circle, and the Chief stepped into the middle of it, where he embarked on a peculiarly grotesque dance. He stretched out his arms horizontally, and began bending and straightening his torso, up and down, up and down, in a sharp, regular rhythm that recalled the movement of a clock's pendulum, slightly speeded up. He wriggled his shoulders and twisted his buttocks about in the most fantastic way. Considering what a great bladder of lard he was, it was astonishing how supple he remained. Every two or three minutes some man would come up to the Chief, interrupt his dance, embrace him, and say: 'Chief, you dance so wonderfully that I can't resist the pleasure of giving you two thousand francs as a token of my appreciation.'

Sometimes the present offered was a pair of sheep, or fifty kilos of cocoa; but everybody came up and offered something or other, and, as each present was declared, the Chief would go and embrace his wife. When I say 'embrace', I mean just that: the Chief would wrap himself round the girl and hold her tightly against him for a considerable time, like the stupid vulgarian he was. During each of these sessions the instruments thudded away louder than ever, and the young people sang a special hymn of praise in honour of their Chief, which I've forgotten, fortunately.

Zambo and I were hugely amused by the whole set-up, and

we spent most of the evening trying to stop ourselves from laughing at the wrong moments. My uncle would give an occasional discreet smile, which could not betray what he was really thinking in the depths of his mind about this particular celebration. In point of fact I've never managed to find out for certain whether my uncle held any precisely definable views on the Chief and his activities.

The Chief was still shimmying away, panting and sweating, but determined not to take off any of his court dress – not even the broad leather belt, which he had done up as tightly as he could. He reminded me of some sergeant-major in the colonial infantry, got up in his number ones for a ceremonial inspection.

By now the room was getting very stuffy and smoke-filled. Suddenly I noticed that Zambo had gone, had, almost literally, vanished. The Chief continued his gyrations, sweat soaking through all over his uniform now; and the drink was beginning to take effect on me.

Zambo returned half an hour later, full of mysterious triumph. He bent over towards me, made sure no one was listening, and whispered: 'Listen, cousin: you're feeling very tired, aren't you?'

'Me? Tired?' I said. 'Certainly not!'

'Yes, yes: you are tired, *very* tired. You've got a headache, too.'

'Are you out of your mind?'

'Ah, don't be so dim. Listen: tell my father that you're feeling tired, and you don't feel very well —'

'But why on earth should I?'

'Ah, go on and do it; don't argue.'

I did as he told me. My uncle passed on the message to the Chief, whispering discreetly in his ear. The Chief stopped dancing, and there was a long pow-wow between him, my uncle, and various members of the 'court'. Finally the Chief beckoned me over, put a large moist paw on my shoulder, and said: 'If you're not feeling well, boy, you'd better go off to bed. I'll send you some nice presents tomorrow. Have a good night's sleep and look after yourself. It's a shame, your getting ill on the first day of the celebrations, but it doesn't really matter. If you take proper care, you'll certainly be all right again before they're over.'

With that he dismissed me. My uncle told Zambo to look sharp and see his poor sick cousin home. We went off slowly, leaving my uncle behind.

As soon as we were alone, Zambo began to chuckle to himself. 'Clever trick, wasn't it?' he said. 'I can't help thinking you'll get more peace and quiet this way.'

I was deeply grateful to him. His whole concern had been to enable me to break out from my encircling prison. But I was to find that Zambo, as usual, had let his zeal push him on to somewhat unseemly extremes. I have become increasingly convinced that my cousin had some kind of Freudian bee in his bonnet – certainly when I think of the obsession he displayed over arranging meetings with women for me. He positively flogged his brain in his efforts to pander me into bed with them. Luckily he wasn't blessed with much imagination, or my visit to Kala would have been one long confused crisis. But on this particular occasion he was entirely successful.

As soon as we were inside my uncle's house, Zambo shooed me off to my room with considerable lack of ceremony. This suprised me at first; in the ordinary way he treated me with great courtesy when I was under their roof. He shut the door on me, told me to wait till he came back, and departed.

I at once realized that he had some idea or other firmly lodged in that thick skull of his, but just what it was I didn't know. To tell the truth, since I had come to know Edima, my urge to accomplish the sexual act in its strict sense had greatly diminished; I had almost forgotten my original desire for 'initiation'. I find it difficult to explain this fact completely. I suppose that my numerous physical contacts with Edima, slight though they were, may have partially relieved me. Besides this, there was the complex, almost contradictory emotion I felt for the girl, because of that it would have been difficult for me to make up my mind to deflower her, just like that. I needed my hearty country cousin to get me out of this subtle dilemma, just as it took Alexander to cut the Gordian knot.

I was still half-stupefied when my cousin returned, dragging Edima by one hand. Poor little Edima! It was difficult to tell whether she had come of her own free will or not, and she probably wasn't sure herself. She seemed both terrified and amused, half-intimidated, half-mocking. How on earth had Zambo worked such a devilish trick? I quickly gave up trying to solve that one.

Without saying a word, Zambo went out again, leaving Edima and me alone together. (I wouldn't be surprised if he stayed with his ear glued to the door, though.) I stared at Edima in dumb misery, while she returned my gaze half-smiling now, one finger in her mouth like a little child being introduced to a stranger. At this point, I remember, I sighed and thought: I may have drunk a good deal, but I'm not really up to the mark yet. I'd better have a drop more.

Aloud I said: 'Sit down, Edima. I haven't seen you for ages. Where have you been all this time?'

I didn't listen to her explanation; while she was talking I bent down under the foot of my bed, pulled out my whisky-bottle, and gulped down several mouthfuls without drawing breath. At once I became far more passionate and excited; it seemed as though this slight alcoholic stimulus had triggered off the dormant effect of all the stuff I had drunk earlier.

Edima sat down on the bed, at a decent distance from me.

'Come here, baby,' I said, playfully.

She shook her head. She wouldn't come any closer. I had to move over to her.

When I was beside her, she turned her head away. I took her hand, and she snatched it away sharply; but this gesture was accompanied by a provocative little laugh that merely encouraged me to go farther. My heart was beating so violently that it felt like some wild animal trying to fight its way out of a cage. I grasped her hand again, and again she nervously pulled it away. I began to get irritated. I seized both her hands at once, and she struggled savagely. I was a bit astonished at her violence, because normally she was such a gentle little creature; but I didn't let go. I wouldn't pretend that I knew how far I wanted to go at that moment. The male nervous system is constructed in such a way that, once it is set in motion, it can't stop till it has reached and passed its climax. The whole thing becomes a matter of mechanical necessity.

We were locked together now in a silent struggle, a struggle the violence of which was only equalled by its total lack of apparent motive. We rolled across the bed; I would never have guessed that so young a girl – even a country peasant – could have exerted such remarkable strength. We fought for a long time. Edima's main endeavour was to scratch me, as if she wanted not only to hurt, but also to mark me. I couldn't understand it. Driven on by whisky and circumstance, I had, as it seemed to me, become an actor in a strange, crazy comedy.

I was more excited than ever. At the very height of the struggle I broke loose, swallowed two or three mouthfuls of whisky, ripped off my shirt as though I was too hot, and flung myself back on Edima to continue the battle. But Edima, her breath coming in deep shuddering gasps, burst out laughing and said: 'No, no, no – I'm too tired – I give in – I don't want to fight any more —'

But I had only just got into my stride.

For days on end the festivities went on in the Chief's house, with drums and xylophones hammering away non-stop, except for the mornings which, not surprisingly, were pretty quiet. Things got going again about one o'clock in the afternoon, and really hotted up after sunset, when the women and girls got back from the fields.

I spent most of this time in my room. Zambo invented an imaginary illness to explain my absence, and even my uncle appeared to believe this flimsy excuse. (Whether he in fact did or not is another matter.) I decided that Zambo was really a sterling character. He not only thought up this providential illness for me, but worked wonders in getting rid of all those kindly souls (Kala swarms with such tiresome busybodies) who wanted to visit the invalid. Only a few younger people, notably that inseparable trio comprising Duckfoot Johnny, the Boneless Wonder, and Son-of-God, actually got in to see me. On these occasions Zambo made sure that it was at a time when there were no prying eyes to fear. The visitors would come into the big sitting-room, and I would then join them from my bedroom: after which (since they knew what was going on) we would have a hearty laugh together. We would frequently empty a large calabash of palm-wine between us, provided out of Duckfoot Johnny's Living Fountains.

Since the feasting went on indefinitely, and monopolized the attention of the whole village, Edima came to see me every evening. We no longer fought; often now we did not even make love. On these occasions Edima and I would sit side by side, arms round each other, and talk for hours. She was fascinated by the idea of the big city, and questioned me endlessly about it. I tried, with very little success, to dissuade her from the idea of ever going there. She, for her part, told me local legends, and sang her native songs for me. One day she sang me the song Duckfoot Johnny had taught me; but she sang it far better than he did, linking each verse to the next *ad infinitum*, in the most skilful fashion. She had an extraordinary memory; one evening she went through no fewer than fifteen verses of this particular song. When she sang it, it wasn't grotesque (as Duckfoot Johnny made it) or even tear-jerking; it was just sad. She loved it.

One evening I asked her why she was so fond of this particular song.

'Because I shall be an orphan myself one day,' she told me. 'All children become orphans sooner or later.'

Curious: Duckfoot Johnny had said almost exactly the same thing. I said: 'It isn't certain that you'll become an orphan; you might well die before your parents. What's to stop you?'

She thought about this for a moment, then shook her head and replied: 'It's true, some children do die before their parents. But it isn't in the least *normal*. In the general way,

137

parents die before their children do.' She hesitated a moment, then went on: 'Anyway, there are thousands of orphans, all over the world. I'm singing for them. Besides, we're all of us orphaned of something – or somebody.'

'What do you mean?'

She laughed. 'When you're gone,' she said, 'I shall be *your* orphan, shan't I?'

This girl is terrible, I thought. There's no doubt about it, she's a real case.

When I look back, and compare what Edima might have become with what actually happened to her, it leaves me dreaming sadly about the imperfections of mankind. A reasonably intelligent fellow – intelligent enough, that is, to interest himself in his fellow men and perhaps even understand them in some degree – could have made her perfectly happy. But the stupidity and mediocrity of human nature in general, and men in particular, decreed otherwise.

Our idyll could not, by the very nature of things, last much longer. Terrestrial paradises are specifically made with the intention of enabling future generations to treat them as legendary.

One evening, in fact, sufficed to spoil everything. Edima had come to see me while dancing was going on at her father's. We had made love with pleasurable violence: she was a very grown-up girl now. There we lay in bed, side by side, chatting about nothing in particular: I forget exactly what. I never got tired of listening to Edima's voice: I found myself exploring the valleys and contours of her mind (to my astonishment) as I would a newly discovered country.

The first thing we heard was the row going on outside. A woman was talking in a very loud and angry voice, while Zambo made unsuccessful attempts to calm her down, muttering under his breath as though ashamed of something.

Edima sat up in bed. 'That's my mother!' she gasped.

'Your *mother*?' I repeated, stupefied.

And at this point the good lady herself burst into the room. She had six or seven rooms to choose from, but she seemed to know by instinct just which one her daughter would be in. She was in a tremendous rage. Zambo had crept in in her wake, probably to make sure she didn't do too much damage.

There was very little room for doubt as to what Edima and I had been doing; we hadn't even had time to put on our clothes again. Edima's mother just stood there, shrieking and swearing all round the clock.

'My God!' she screamed, 'look at this! My own daughter – a child, a mere infant – in bed with a man! Oh, Lord, have mercy on me! What a wretched unhappy woman I am! My own daughter, and it seems only yesterday I bore her! Couldn't this – this town rake find anything more mature in the whole village?' Then she turned to Edima. 'Get up, you shameless hussy,' she bellowed, 'you strumpet, you fallen woman! I don't know what your father and I have done to deserve such a child —' And so on, *ad infinitum*.

Then she grabbed Edima by one hand, and hauled her out of bed stark naked. Zambo kept making rather perfunctory attempts to pacify her, as though he didn't believe a word she was saying. His attitude surprised and rather annoyed me. Edima's mother was now beating her daughter, still screaming curses between each blow. It looked as though she was going to drag poor Edima out into the street without a stitch on.

'Come on, out with you!' she cried. 'Let the whole village see you as you are now, and learn just what kind of a girl you are!'

'Mama,' begged Edima, weeping, 'Mama, please forgive me – please, please! At least,' she added, 'let me get dressed.'

Her mother granted this small concession, but never drew breath all the time. 'Went off every evening, eh, the little tart! And I thought she was playing games with girls of her own age! But now I come to think of it she's never behaved like a normal girl —' (She was talking now as though enrolling my cousin and myself as witnesses.) 'No, never. I've tried to keep an eye on her, but I've got five children and I can't keep them all out of mischief. If someone had come and told me that Edima was sleeping with a man, do you know what I should have done?'

We said nothing. 'No? I should have killed him. I wouldn't have believed it if I hadn't seen it with my own eyes. Oh, my God!'

I made no attempt to defend Edima; I lay rooted to the bed. It wasn't through cowardice; I've never been a coward, and God forbid I ever should be. I was simply overwhelmed.

She went out, dragging her daughter roughly behind her, and still breathing fire and slaughter as she left. But in our country, luckily, it's difficult to make a real scandal out of such a situation.

When we were alone together, Zambo burst out laughing: a sincere, hearty guffaw.

'Christ, what's so funny?' I asked, in some irritation.

He went on laughing for some time without answering. At last he calmed down and deigned to give me a reply.

'Do you mean to say you don't understand —?'

'Understand *what*?'

'That the whole thing's a carefully planned farce?'

I gaped at him, repeating the phrase.

'Certainly, dear boy. A complete farce. You don't know Kala women. Let me explain. They're all as vain as peacocks, the lot of them —'

'What's that got to do with it?'

'Everything. That old bag simply wanted to be able to tell the whole village that it was *her* daughter you'd honoured with your – h'm – attentions. That whole little scene was pure eyewash.'

'You're barmy, Zambo!'

'Oh, no, I'm not, believe you me. I was born and bred in these parts, and I know something about this kind of caper. You don't need to worry about Edima. Did you see *how* she was beating the kid? Pulling her punches like mad, and trying to make each smack sound as loud as possible at the same time. Tell you something else, too: she'll spend the whole night coddling Edima, to make up for all this fake rough stuff.'

I sat up in bed and said: 'That's a queer way to behave.'

'Oh, that's the way they are, these women. That's how it goes.'

There was a pause. Then Zambo went on: 'And what's so queer about it, anyway? Mothers always want their daughters to get married, don't they? Think it over.'

'You mean – you mean she wants to make me marry Edima?'

'Something of that, I shouldn't wonder.'

I had never seriously considered the idea of marrying Edima. I couldn't quite define the curious feeling it gave me. At first blush it was rather as if someone had told me that I'd just been made a bishop or a general, or something improbable of that sort. Marry Edima: well, well, well.

I said, chewing the notion over: 'How does she reckon she's going to *make* me marry Edima, anyway?'

'We'll find out soon enough. Don't be impatient.'

The idea of marrying a girl doesn't merely prove that you love her. Put it another way: if you *really* love her, however much you may jib at the thought of marriage, sooner or later you resign yourself to it. An impending marriage reveals your true personality. Some people, artists and men of action in particular, think of eventual marriage (whether they are in love or not) as an intolerable drag or burden. Others consider it an essential ingredient for their full development: these are the home-comfort lovers, the fireside-and-slippers brigade, all those who, sooner or later, embrace the middle-aged bourgeois ideal. At the thought of marrying Edima I found that I belonged to the first category: not in a conscious way, but vaguely and obscurely, as seems appropriate in the present day and age.

All that night I thought over both sides of the problem. It would be fun to marry Edima and spend all my time with her. But what on earth would I find to do after a while? We wouldn't make love non-stop. Wouldn't I go potty occasionally if she didn't leave me to myself? What *did* one do with a wife – what, to be more personal, would *I* do with *mine*?

I got very little sleep that night, trying to make up my mind whether I would, in fact, marry Edima if the proposal was made to me. By the morning I had decided, not only to marry her if I was asked, but to demand her hand if her parents omitted to suggest such a course themselves. As to what I should do afterwards, I made up my mind to take that fence when I come to it. And thereby, I thought, would hang a tale and a half.

Edima. How ridiculous the whole business is! I don't mean Edima herself, but the whole silly story as I'm recalling it now: life, in fact. Life is essentially ridiculous. You don't realize how ridiculous it is when you're plunged in it up to the neck, as though it were some viscous, gluey bog. When you struggle free and see it in perspective, it's another matter.

Edima. My brother had often remarked, with that peculiar cynicism characteristic of young people who have had too much experience of women too young: 'What on earth good is it for two virgins to go to bed together? They'll only fumble around and make a nonsense of it. Not once only, either, but time after time. Sometimes they'll go on fumbling for the rest of their lives: that often happens, I'm told.'

You were wrong in our case, my dear brother: Edima and I had no need for fumbling, and yet, I will swear, she was as much a virgin as I was. We did not have to spend years searching for each other, trying to make contact: we hit it off with a bang the very first time. I know the discovery of two bodies truly made for each other, two minds perfectly attuned, is a miracle, a real miracle. No; there was no fumbling between Edima and me.

Edima, Edima – sharp and fresh as a ripening orange, crisp and resilient when bitten: an orange, a green mango, young fruit to be plucked by me alone.

The following morning Duckfoot Johnny, the Boneless Wonder, and Son-of-God came round to the house and – with Zambo to egg them on – had a good laugh at my little adventure. In particular, they passed a large number of comments and made several jokes which confirmed my cousin's theory that the whole thing had been a put-up job.

The younger generation got a good laugh out of the affair; but their elders disregarded it completely. Their attitude to me remained exactly the same: they still showed me great respect, and continued to lavish hospitality on me. I had been going through agonies, expecting to be socially ostracized at the very least; but obviously I had all my worries for nothing. Even my uncle's amiability showed no signs of cooling off.

It was at this stage in the proceedings, before I had even had time to get my personal emotions quietened down a little – let alone sorted out – that my Helen, the real object of my mission, for whom I had been prepared to fight a second Troy before the walls of Kala, appeared on the scene. In other words, Niam's wife, most unexpectedly, returned to the village.

I had been frequently told that men always get the women they deserve. In the normal way of things I distrust such popular saws and village adages like the plague; but I was forced into agreement with this particular one the day Niam's wife appeared. My conversion, to be sure, did not take place immediately on her arrival, since I couldn't then conceive that the man accompanying her was actually her lover; it happened a few hours later, when their true relationship had become common gossip throughout the village.

Now the idea of Niam being cuckolded was quite in character; what infuriated me was that his wife must have known perfectly well that I was waiting for her in her own village. Everyone would have told her during her peregrinations; she was never more than a few miles from Kala. Notwithstanding, she had had the nerve to enter Kala in this scandalous fashion, and in broad daylight at that.

My mother, to whom I recounted this episode, is of the opinion that the scandal was deliberately calculated: that Niam's wife wanted to make it quite clear, not only to me but to our whole tribe, that she might not be a queen, but she was still *someone*, in her own right, not a mere cypher – and that in any case she wasn't short of men. This was the meaning of the scandal as far as my mother was concerned.

If this hypothesis of my mother's holds water – as I think it does – could it not be said that Niam had won after all? What was it he had said? – that he was the earth, and she nothing but a dead leaf fluttering down from some tall tree? Well, if you looked more closely into his wife's provocative actions and desire for revenge, didn't they reveal not only her resentment at not having been treated better by him, but above all the desire to *make him get her back*?

In my opinion, Niam's wife was certainly not lacking in effrontery. I could hardly have demanded fidelity from her; after all, she wasn't *my* wife. But I could and did expect rather more discreetness. It was Zambo who turned up late that afternoon with the news that Niam's wife was accompanied by her lover – the man she had been living with while I waited around for her. I reflected, in some mortification, on the ridiculous position into which I had been manœuvred.

'Besides,' Zambo went on in a mildly disgusted voice, 'besides, she knew very well that you were here. She must have found out weeks ago. She wanted to run you around a bit, that's what it was.'

I asked him if he knew what she'd been up to.

'Knew what? That she was with a man? Of course I knew *that*. These little pushovers are all the same. I knew she must be screwing around with some man or other, but I couldn't be sure that it was this one.'

'You mean it might have been someone else?'

'There were at least three possibles —'

'Good Lord,' I said, inadequately.

'All the women here run two or three men besides their husband when they get to her age. It's practically a rule.'

'Good Lord!' I said again. I was beginning to feel a queer kind of anger. 'Anyway, that solves the problem for me.'

'The problem? What problem?'

'I shall leave tomorrow or the day after,' I said. 'Very soon, anyway.'

'Yes,' Zambo said, 'you'll leave, of course – but with the girl you came here to find, I fancy. First of all there'll be a long palaver with the Chief. That always happens in this sort of affair. My father has gone to lodge an official complaint, in your name —'

'*In my name?*'

'Sure, sure. You don't need to give a damn about the whole thing yourself. Let the old man get on with it.'

'Well, whatever they decide, I can't take this woman back with me. She's too filthy for me to stomach. God, she makes me want to throw up.'

He began to laugh, but stopped himself immediately. 'She may be the slut you say she is,' he said. 'But her husband needs her to run his house, cook his food, and work his fields for him. That's what really matters. You haven't been sent here to judge whether this cow is a slut or not. Your job is simply to take her back, and that's that.'

There was a good deal of common sense in Zambo's remarks: he was more level-headed about the whole thing than I was. Already he viewed life as his ancestors had done, without a trace of either illusion or ambition. It was as though he had decided from the day of his birth that treachery and sluttishness were one's everyday portion, and that it was folly to expect anything else. It struck me that the books which embody this kind of philosophy are always written by old men. But for Zambo, as for all his countrymen, this was no discovery to be made in late middle age, but a living reality in which they were steeped from the cradle to the grave. This unshakeable stoicism in the face of all life's accidents and vicissitudes is probably the townsman's greatest loss, when he abandons village, tribe and local culture. We who choose the city have lost this ancient wisdom: irritable, ambitious, hotheaded, fed on illusion, we have become the world's eternal dupes.

That evening my uncle said to me, over the dinner-table: 'You and I are going to pay a call on the Chief, right away.'

'Why should we do that?' I asked aggressively.

Hitherto I had shown too much passive acquiescence; I had let myself be pushed around as events or people dictated. Now that I realized this, and wanted to shake off so irksome a role, I tended to become aggressive through plain maladroitness. My uncle took some time before replying, but at last he remarked that my wife had arrived.

'My *wife*?' I repeated, incredulously.

'Yes, your wife,' my uncle said, with the air of a teacher squaring up to explain a difficult question to some particularly pin-headed pupil. 'Niam's wife is temporarily yours also. You are not in Kala simply as Niam's representative, but as an emissary from your whole tribe. You must speak with due authority.'

There was a long pause while he swallowed a glass of water. Then he said: 'I gather you haven't the least idea what sort of line you ought to take?'

'No,' I said, 'none whatsoever.'

'Listen, my boy. This woman arrived here in the company of a man. That's an open scandal. It's scandalous because she's still Niam's wife – there hasn't been any divorce – and she's still got Niam's dowry; she goes around wearing it, in fact. Therefore a misdemeanour has been committed by the man for borrowing her as a wife, even if only for a few days. He owes you damages, compensation, see?'

I began to wonder what sort of a cut my uncle would get out of this new deal. As though reading my thoughts he said, without looking at me: 'Do you understand what I mean?'

'Not entirely. For instance, I don't see just what sort of compensation this man owes me. If it comes to that, I don't know him, and have no particular wish to make his acquaintance.'

My uncle said: 'It doesn't matter whether you know him or not. The important thing is that he's been intimate with – er – your wife. He owes you compensation, either in cash or kind, as you prefer. The exact amount will be fixed by the Chief during the palaver.'

I said, tentatively: 'I suppose – if this man does make me some financial reparation, that is – that I'll take the money back to Niam. After all, it's his wife, isn't it?'

'If you so desire, you're quite at liberty to take the money

146

home with you for Niam. But according to our customs, you have every right to keep it for yourself, as a reward for the mission you have undertaken. Look on it as expenses, h'm? Reimbursement for all the trouble you've been put to.'

I failed to see what trouble the mission had put me to so far, but this I refrained from observing to my uncle.

"All right then: we'll go and see the Chief right away,' my uncle said, in a brisk, decisive voice. 'You'd better let me do the talking; you don't know our customs very well yet. Just listen, and learn,'

O.K., I thought; I'll do just that.

Zambo agreed to come with us to the Chief's house. The festivities were over now, but they had left a nostalgic kind of memory behind, like a fine summer evening, or a field the day after it's been harvested. The bridal delegation had gone home; yet when we entered the big reception-room we found it packed. Every elder in Kala seemed to be present, not to mention a considerable sprinkling of young girls.

I didn't see anything unusual at first in the elders being there: after all, there was a matter to be decided, the affair of Niam's wife, which involved an appeal to tribal custom. But all these girls puzzled me. I racked my brains trying to work out what they were doing there, and above all why there was this festive air about them, as though there was another marriage to be celebrated, a second bride to deliver to her husband.

At first things went off with almost disconcerting ease – so easily, in fact, that I was taken a little off my guard. The Chief handed out the quickest and most expeditious justice I've ever seen dispensed in my life. The two accused were sent for, and appeared immediately. When she came in, Niam's wife walked across and shook me by the hand. I returned her greeting coldly; I had already conceived a violent distaste for her, which doubled in intensity when I got a good look at her lover. He was a stupid, gaping clod of a peasant, and as ugly as sin: so ugly, in fact, that if he had once turned up in my home-town, the whole affair would promptly have become a kind of legend.

It occurred to me that if one of these two had really gone after the other, had made provocative advances and all the rest of it, it must have been Niam's wife. You only had to look at the man to see that he wouldn't ever dream of seducing anybody, let alone Niam's wife, who was not lacking in a certain crude charm.

Soon after their entry, the Chief announced his intention of speaking. A chorus of *shushes* ran round the room. Everyone stopped talking.

The Chief made a brief speech, outlining the course of the affair in a couple of sentences. He was by no means lacking in either clarity or eloquence; it was clear that he had some experience in the art of administering justice, even if in a somewhat summary fashion. As he said, there were two sides to this affair: first, Niam's quarrel with his wife; secondly, a case of flagrant adultery.

'We'll come back to the marital quarrel in a moment,' the Chief said. 'This woman is still Niam's wife in the eyes of the law: there has been no divorce, and Niam's dowry – which young Jean-Marie Medza is here to protect – has not been repaid.'

At this point the Chief broke off to whisper various private orders to two of his girls, who had been sitting beside him awaiting his orders. Then he went on: 'We will deal first with the adultery, which is flagrant and undeniable. There's no difficulty about this part of it. The guilty party will pay to the injured husband, represented here by Jean-Marie Medza, such a sum as the law lays down in such cases. This sum, as you are all aware, amounts to two thousand francs. The payment must be made by this evening. According to the regulations, the co-respondent can offer four grown rams or two young ewes in lieu of cash, if he is without liquid funds. That is all. I call you to witness, my brothers, that this is a just judgement.'

There was a long murmur of approval from everyone present. The co-respondent was slumped in is chair, looking neither more nor less stupefied than he had on his first appearance. Poor devil: two thousand francs, or four healthy rams, or two young ewes – it was no laughing matter to him. I felt sorry for him: I felt that he had been victimized – and so, of course, he had. It was obviously Niam's wife who had taken the initiative in the whole affair, and got him tangled up in these disastrous proceedings.

The Chief once more broke off to whisper orders to two more girls, who were sitting – or, more accurately, squatting – at his feet. It looked as if some little plot were being hatched. I thought the Chief might be arranging for me to be brought the presents he had promised me, but which hadn't so far arrived.

'Now let us turn to the essential part of the matter,' he resumed. 'In the old days, our ancestors took no cognisance of certain customs now common among us today. Our ancestors did not admit the possibility of a wife leaving her husband. But since then the white men have come here; they have decreed that a wife *may* leave her husband, always on the condition that she returns his dowry. My personal opinion is that such a law is iniquitous; it turns women into disobedient, rebellious wives. But what can I do? It is the law, and in my capacity as your Chief, I must administer it scrupulously.'

He turned to Niam's wife. 'Woman: is it your firm intention to leave your husband, to obtain what they call a "divorce"? Tell us now. Speak out so that we can all hear your words, and know exactly what it is you want.'

Niam's wife, as I have said, was by no means lacking in effrontery. She launched into a long rambling speech, without, however, giving any real details of her quarrel with her husband. The point of this exercise remained extremely obscure, since in the end she declared herself ready to return to him. The Chief, who was indifferent to her wiles, cut her short and said, turning to me: 'Monsieur Jean-Marie Medza, here is the woman you came to find. You can take her away with you whenever you like.'

That concluded the proceedings. The Chief invited my uncle, Zambo, and myself to dinner. My uncle said we had eaten already; the Chief replied that we could at least keep him company while he had his meal. We went through into the dining-room, a large, airy chamber. The table was already laid, and the meal waiting. Before he began his dinner, the Chief told the people in the reception-room not to go away, as the evening was only just beginning.

Then he sat down and began to gorge himself with disgusting abandon, although his new wife was also present at table. The rest of us just nibbled a few mouthfuls out of politeness.

Afterwards we returned to the reception-room. There then began the finest comic performance I have ever seen in my life; one, moreover, in which I played a leading role. It was a play in one act and three scenes; and its plot-line developed with relentless precision.

First of all, the Chief ordered the young girls to begin dancing. They formed a circle in the middle of the big room and performed a dance remarkable for its lightness and elegance, singing and clapping their hands rhythmically all the time. Each girl in turn slipped into the centre of the circle and performed solo for a few moments, then gave place to the next in line. It was, as Zambo agreed, all very easy on the eye.

Then a motley collection of people swarmed in, some carrying musical instruments – the usual drums, tom-toms, and xylophones – others staggering under demi-johns of palm-wine or claret. The demi-johns were made of clear glass, and you could see the wine jumping and frothing inside. The guests, old men mostly, at once began to drink; and my uncle, Zambo, and I joined them. Things hotted up very quickly. The Chief was in a jovial, almost hilarious mood, which I put down without a second's thought to the presence of his new wife.

The only thing that worried me was Edima's absence. I began to wonder about Zambo's common-sense reassurances. If Edima wasn't present this evening, I thought, it could only be because she had been closely chaperoned since being discovered in my bedroom.

Then the Chief entered the lists himself and began to dance with the girls. The drums and tom-toms beat out exactly the same rhythms as they had done the day the bridal delegation arrived in Kala. I shot a furtive glance at my uncle: he was relaxed and smiling, cheerful enough to all appearances. Zambo, on the other hand, despite a certain air of superficial amusement, was as detached as ever. There was a hubbub of conversation going on in the room, but I couldn't make out the drift of their remarks, nor, indeed, exactly what they were talking about: this was chiefly because they had split up into little groups and, as far as I could gather, each group was arguing about something different.

Anyway, there was the same stupefying din going on outside as there had been during the bridal delegation's visit. I felt extremely nervous, mostly because I felt I was losing my grip on events. The Chief's new wife was here in the room with us; so what on earth were these new junketings in aid of? Zambo hadn't said a word, so obviously he wasn't any wiser than I was. I glanced at him, and saw the same bafflement clearly registered in his face.

The usual procession of women was coming slowly up the steps: by now I was positively panting with curiosity. They advanced in leisurely fashion as far as the doorway, then defiled into the room itself. In the middle of the procession walked a bewildered, frightened, shame-faced girl, a girl of about the same age as Edima —

My God, it *was* Edima.

There was no mistaking her: this girl was Edima all right, my own little Edima. There she stood, eyes modestly lowered, while all round her the other women yodelled and screeched away fit to burst my eardrums. I was hypnotized by this tableau: I stared at it, unable to remove my gaze, fixed in helpless concentration. I must have half-stood up in my armchair. For several long moments I had no conscious thoughts: I was thrown back on my senses alone, like a primitive living creature, or a tropical flower touched by the first rays of the sun.

When I regained my senses, I saw that the Chief had taken Edima by the hand, and was coming over in my direction, trailing his daughter behind him. Now he was joining our hands together. He followed up this gesture with a long speech. I don't recall a word of it today; I only know that it was the exact counterpart, the twin brother, so to speak, of the speech made a day or two before by the leader of the bridal delegation.

After this he made Edima and myself sit down side by side. As far as I remember, Edima kept her eyes lowered. For my own part, I probably didn't do anything so modest; all the same, I quite certainly didn't see a thing at the time. I shall always remember the silent gesture which Zambo made when these alarming ceremonies began: he slid his arm through mine, as though to give me something to lean on, and as an earnest that he would never abandon me, in whatever trouble I might be.

Even all these years afterwards I still don't feel that I have ever quite repaid my cousin for this one gesture. When I wonder why we have remained so closely united, such intimate friends, I sometimes fancy that that moment explains the whole thing.

Zambo leaned over and whispered in my ear: 'I told you, didn't I? I knew damned well they'd hitch you up with their daughter. I never thought they'd go about it this way, though.'

He poured me out a glass of red wine, and I swallowed it at a single gulp. I was beginning to understand what was happening. I have to confess that the more I thought about it, the happier I felt – though, naturally, a little put out by the circumstances.

At this point the Chief flung himself into another solo dance. It was just as frenzied as the one he had performed a few days before, and no less difficult to analyse or describe. The drums thundered round him; occasionally he would interrupt his gyrations to announce the presents he proposed making to his new son-in-law. The list grew a little longer each time. This wild dance was also interrupted by organized interludes, during which the girls sang a celebratory song, to the same tune as their previous effort, in honour of the Chief. But on this occasion – although they never mentioned me by name – *I* was the subject of their delicate and flattering allusions. They enumerated a whole catalogue of rare qualities I was deemed to possess, and very proud I should have been of myself if I actually had them. I was struck by their facility in improvising verse couplets to go with a familiar tune. Everybody meanwhile gazed at me with open admiration and a little envy, as one does with a man who's just had a notable stroke of luck.

To the best of my recollection, my uncle made a speech at some point during this unforgettable evening (as it may well be described); I fancy he was all enthusiasm. Oddly enough, I don't remember a word he said; but no more would anyone else in my position, if you ask me. I do recall that he got drunk – a rare occurrence indeed. Zambo told me it was only the third time it had happened, to his knowledge.

The junketings went on till daybreak, and it was only then that I was allowed to go to bed. The Chief said: 'Go and sleep it off, boy. You can come and get your wife tomorrow night. She'll sleep by your side from then on. You won't have anything to worry about in the future, will you, eh?' and he burst into a huge wheezing laugh. It was a kindly enough remark, but how that laugh infuriated me!

My uncle whispered reassuringly in my ear: 'Don't worry about anything. I've got the whole situation in hand.'

He had the situation so well in hand, as it turned out, that Niam's wife's boy-friend was called upon to discharge his fine as soon as I had gone. Though he was far from his own village, he wasn't entirely without friends in Kala: as a result he managed to borrow two ewes to settle his account with the law. He preferred, as might have been expected, to deal in kind rather than cash. The two ewes in question were added to the enormous flock already milling round my uncle's pens. That was what he meant by having the situation in hand.

I was half-dead with lack of sleep when I got back to my room. Wearily I asked Zambo what he thought I should do now.

'How do you mean?' he asked.

'In the present situation,' I said.

'Nothing. Your job's over. What do you want to do, anyway?'

'Oh, can't you understand? What on earth am I going to do with this girl?'

'Edima? That's all right, she's your wife, isn't she? What more do you want?'

For a while I was consumed with a strange angry bitterness. Why, I asked myself, couldn't things in the last resort be as easy as Zambo pictured them?

'You look a proper misery,' Zambo said. 'What are you thinking about?'

'Do you know my father?' I asked.

'I've met him three or four times —'

'That's not what I meant. Do you know what sort of man he is?'

'Well, no, I suppose not.'

'He'll tan the hide off me for this,' I said.

'But why? Because you've got married? All you need to tell him is that you were hijacked into it under false pretences —'

'He'll do worse than beat me; he'll make my whole future life absolute hell. It's all my bloody elder brother's fault —'

'Eh? Why?'

'I tell you it's so. If my elder brother hadn't been such a bonehead, my father would have worked off all his frustrated ambitions on *him*. As things are, the old boy has to torment me instead —'

I yawned, and before I could develop this melancholy line of thought any further, I was fast asleep.

I woke late in the afternoon, to hear snatches of conversation drifting through from the living-room. Draping my robe about me, I went out to investigate, and found Duckfoot Johnny, the Boneless Wonder, Son-of-God, Zambo, and several other young men gathered there.

'Well, well, he's awake at last,' said Duckfoot Johnny. 'We were beginning to wonder if you'd died the day after your wedding.'

I was still in a half-doped state, so said nothing.

'Wouldn't have minded a slice off that cake myself,' Son-of-God put in. 'But what a crafty old goat her father is! Ever since Jean-Marie turned up in Kala, I bet the old devil's only had one idea in his head – to marry Edima off to him. Lucky that Edima's a nice girl, anyway – best fledgling in the nest, when you look at the others. But what's her dad going to get out of it? What's in it for him? That's what I still don't see.'

'Don't be so dim,' Zambo said. 'He reckons he'll have someone in the city now to help him with his dirty business deals – a real educated gent into the bargain. And he won't sit around here the whole time, either. You wait and see: he'll always be off on visits to his daughter or his son-in-law. He loves inviting himself around as a guest of honour. Some people are silly enough to think he's generous; but the only people he lays himself out for are those who can do him a rather bigger favour in return. Before my cousin arrived, that old sod never even knew of my father's existence. The name of Mama meant nothing to him. But as soon as Jean-Marie appeared, he began smarming round my father like mad, the dirty little greaser.'

'What about us?' said Duckfoot Johnny. 'He thinks we're a bad lot, so *we* don't get any invitations out of him.'

'Well, we don't exactly cherish *him*, come to that,' said the Boneless Wonder. His time spent teaching children their catechism had left him certain elementary notions of charity.

'There are plenty more who don't exactly cherish him,' said Son-of-God, 'but they get invited nevertheless.'

'Anyway,' Duckfoot Johnny concluded, 'if he *did* invite me, I shouldn't go. I'm a damn sight better off at home with my palm-wine, a nice bit of roast antelope, and a yam or two. The hell with all Chiefs and their parties!'

'The Chief,' said the Boneless Wonder, as charitable as ever, 'the Chief is a poor, pitiable creature really, my friends; a mere bubble of vanity.'

'Ah, the hell with him, anyway,' said Duckfoot Johnny, and signalled to Son-of-God, who extracted from under a cane-bottomed chair a huge swag-bellied calabash, brimming with palm-wine.

'This is to celebrate your marriage,' he announced, without a trace of irony.

We drank the first round in silence. Then Duckfoot Johnny asked me if would stay a few more days in Kala.

'I don't know,' I said. 'I can't tell at the moment.'

'Hurry up and find out, chum. I'll tell you why: if you've got a day or so more here, we'll lay on a party for your marriage, a real hell of a party, something to remember us by.'

He paused, and then went on: 'I gather you don't know what to do with your wife, h'm? My dear fellow, you don't know how lucky you are. Have you any idea what a wife normally costs these days? A small fortune, no kidding. Take my case: look what's happened to me since I gave up trying to get married. You know what I'm going to do now? I'm going to get me a real old bag, a squeezed orange of a woman – a widow, or some middle-aged tart everyone's had a bash at. That way I'll make a cheaper deal, and it's better than nothing.'

'Compare your position with mine, though. You get a wife for sweet damn all – you don't even have to go and chase her, she comes to you. And what a wife, brother, what a wife! Young, *really* young, with that fresh, healthy adolescent bloom – like a brand-new pair of shoes in a Greek shop. Though come to think of it, I've never seen a new pair of shoes in a Greek shop, at that. You don't know your luck, you really don't. As for your father, what's the odds if he beats you or plays merry hell with your life? Fundamentally you can snap your fingers at him; you've got a real little treasure of your own. Don't let him run you around.'

He drank deeply, and repeated: 'Find out if you'll still be here for another four or five days. We want to give you a really terrific party. You won't forget us, we'll see to that.'

Unfortunately, this party never took place; because that same evening I told my uncle that I wanted to go home to my own village. The urge descended upon me very suddenly. Much in the same way an alcoholic, after a brief interlude during which his drink-sodden stomach heaves at the very thought of liquor, will suddenly return to his vice once more.

'Well, boy, if you want to go home to your father, there's nothing to stop you, is there? When do you intend leaving?'

'The day after tomorrow.'

'That's quite all right: the day after tomorrow will do very well.'

We decided all the important details on the spot. The main thing was the division of the flock: we decided to share rams and ewes in equal proportions, leaving me half of each. My uncle went on for ages about getting the exact numbers right, which didn't interest me in the least. Then he came to the difficult part of the business. About a fortnight after my departure, a delegation from Kala would deliver my wife to me, and he, my uncle, would without doubt come with them. He would take advantage of this trip to transport my share of the cattle and poultry – not to mention Niam's wife.

I said I hoped Zambo would come too.

'Take him with you if you like,' said my uncle without hesitation. 'You might be able to make something out of him.'

'You really mean it?' I said in some astonishment, 'I can really take him with me?'

'Surely, surely – take him by all means if you want to!'

It occurred to me that in all probability Zambo himself would not want to leave Kala. I went off to sound him on this important point, and he was enthusiastic beyond my most sanguine hopes. We were both as delighted as a pair of schoolboys after hearing that the holidays have been put forward and there won't be any classes tomorrow. I wasn't quite sure why I was so anxious for Zambo to come back home with me. It may have been to repay some of the kindness he had shown me during my stay; it may, on the other hand, have been merely selfish – using his presence to bolster up my courage when I faced my father after all these escapades. Anyway, I was as pleased as could be.

But my uncle at once dampened my joy by saying: 'Listen, my boy, I'm only too glad for Zambo to come with you, but I can't let him go the day after tomorrow: I need him to work a few more days in the coconut-plantation. He can come at the same time as the delegation, with me. It's his own fault entirely. If he worked properly and didn't play hookey the whole time, he'd have finished his job in the plantation by now and would be free to go where he liked. But I've told you before, he's the laziest, most good-for-nothing creature that's ever existed.'

We abruptly put our joy away again. It was rather like sheathing your sword when there hasn't been a fight after all. But we didn't give up hope entirely.

That evening the Chief sent for me and Zambo. We arrived at his house together, and he made us take dinner with him. He asked me if I had received his presents. I said I had, and thanked him in the prescribed fashion.

'Don't thank me,' he said. 'A son ought never to thank his father. As from yesterday, you're my son – since you married my daughter, in fact. You see, I realized right from the beginning that you and she were in love with each other. So I said to myself, we'll do something really magnificent; we'll marry these two children – they're in love already. I hope you'll both always feel about each other as you do now. It does me good to look at you both' – I forgot to say that Edima was there too, sitting next to me – 'and I'll pay you frequent visits. I'm sure your father will be delighted with this turn of events, especially when he hears that Edima is my daughter.'

We went back home, taking Edima with us.

Her mood betrayed neither misery nor elation, but simply a certain astonishment, and a nervous timidity she had never shown before to such a degree. I racked my brains to find a motive for this sudden recrudescence of her earlier fears.

While she slept, I watched her closely. Edima, my wife. I was in a fine state of perplexity; I was no longer capable of understanding my own reactions – not that I had ever been very clear about them. My own personality confronted me, rather like a boisterous child that has suddenly grown up. Such a child is beyond the reach of its parents; they can't stop it going ahead faster and faster, they can't cradle it in their arms. It struggles against them, and by now its strength is such that it breaks loose from their restraining grasp and goes its own way.

I should have done something which in fact I had not: a comparatively simple act in itself. I ought to have told the Chief that he had made a mistake: that I couldn't and wouldn't marry his daughter. What was I afraid of? I had been taken by surprise. After the first momentary shock I ought to have pulled myself together and taken a strong line with this ass of a Chief. But I hadn't done it. The worst of it was that when I could still have acted in this way I chose not to – not through resignation but by deliberate choice. Quite deliberate. I know you'll tell me I'm deceiving myself again, fudging my motives. But I really believe that I didn't want to let Edima go, that this was a perfectly conscious decision. Even today I feel that my decision would be the same. Unfortunately, it's a bit too late now, but never mind about that.

You'll also tell me, I don't doubt, that I shouldn't have acted in a way that caused poor little Edima suffering: but this line will hardly stand overmuch inspection. I don't know if you've ever been in mortal terror of your father. Imagine a defenceless adolescent whose father has always been in his eyes a terrible and omnipotent god. (So I believed at the time, certainly; but it had already become less true for me, even since my journey to Kala.) What weight has the desire not to hurt a girl's feelings when set in the scale beside the fear of incurring Jove's own thunderous wrath?

As I lay there beside Edima, everything, even my father's

temper, seemed suddenly of negligible importance. I even contrived to feel a certain sneaking sympathy with the Chief, simply because he was Edima's father: that'll show you. In short, I was in love with Edima. That may seem silly to you, but I can't help it. I was in love with this girl; and as a result, I was reaching a state of mind in which I either couldn't see or systematically ignored the relentless, inevitable pattern of my real existence. That, I suppose, is what we mean by love: a condition in which the possible and impossible alike appear as attributes of a wholly mythical universe invented by some imaginary Fairy Carabosse. When *that* happens, it's sure proof that you're in love. A fat lot you worry then about what your father will think, or how your future way of life, your natural temperament, or whatever, will square up to this great love of yours.

Edima lay asleep beside me, her right arm pillowing her head. Her face was serene and innocent; her breathing gentler than a kitten's. There was nothing real or concrete about her: her whole person evoked a dream of the ideal, the intangible, the unattainable.

How bizarre the whole affair is, I thought.

The following day – the day before my departure from Kala, that is – as dusk was falling my uncle took me through the village to pay brief farewell visits, especially on those heads of families who had entertained me. They lavished advice and blessings on me with great generosity, nearly all saying exactly the same thing in exactly the same fashion: they wore identical expressions, their general attitude and homely wisdom came off the same peg in every case. It was all madly boring.

We visited the Chief last of all, and he said very little: merely reminded me that he would pay a visit on us very shortly, for the express reason of meeting my father.

There was a frankly sentimental scene on the morning of my departure. All the girls and women in Kala wanted to shake hands with me before going off to the fields. It goes without saying that the kiddies didn't want to be left out, either.

You'll come back and see us soon, won't you? The question was asked again and again, without respite.

'I don't know,' I replied. 'I don't know. Yes, I'll certainly come back some time. But I don't know when.'

'You'll be good to our little Edima, won't you?'

'Be good to her,' someone else said, 'she's very young still – a child, a mere baby really —'

'Of course I'll be good to her,' I said.

'Oh, you people *down there*, in the big city – we've heard all about you, how casually you abandon your wives. You won't desert Edima, will you?'

'I promise you I won't desert her,' I said.

The hands stretched out to grasp mine, an endless queue of them.

Finally I said good-bye to my uncle, his wife, and Zambo's girl-friend. These two women had been so self-effacing that I had hardly been aware of their existence during my stay in Kala.

My bicycle had been thoroughly cleaned and oiled the previous evening by Zambo, who had appointed himself to this task with great pride.

The younger folk accompanied me as far as the forest track beyond the village. There was Duckfoot Johnny, the Boneless Wonder, Son-of-God, Zambo, Endongolo, and a few more whose names I have forgotten. It goes without saying that Edima came with them too.

They all said more or less the same thing to me: 'I'll probably come and visit you in town one day, boy. I won't warn you, I'll just turn up like a chimpanzee out of the jungle. I only hope you'll recognize me.'

And I would reply: 'Of course I'll recognize you, old friend. How could I ever not recognize you?'

I held Edima's hand in mine all the time. She, in contrast to the rest, was silent throughout: she knew that in a fortnight we should be together again. Zambo, who was wheeling my bicycle for me, hardly said a word either.

As we approached the red, dusty track, and the moment of departure hung over us, Duckfoot Johnny said: 'It's a pity we never had time for that final party. But it doesn't matter, we'll keep it for next time. You'll probably forget us very quickly, but we'll always remember you. If the Chief tries to rope you in on his dirty little games – anything that could possibly compromise a decent human being – tell him to go stuff himself: that'd be the best possible way of proving that you haven't forgotten us.'

I shook hands with them all, kissed Edima on the forehead, and mounted my bicycle. Before they passed out of sight round a bend in the track, I looked round once and waved to them. They stood there motionless, the whole group, bang in the middle of the road. If the tears did not spring to my eyes now, it was simply because since the previous evening I had no longer been with them in spirit: I was at home once more, caught back into the powerful orbit of my father.

CHAPTER FOUR

In which at last — and not without a slight feeling of relief — the reader will learn the real conclusion of this story — a conclusion all too predictable, alas, despite what may have been suggested to the contrary.

Here let me offer certain suggestions guaranteed to remove all ambiguities and misunderstandings. If the reader is a virtuous paterfamilias, instead of taking offence at some of the reflections here set forth (which in any case must be treated with some reserve), he ought to bear in mind that these events are, after all, fiction, and remember that the author has already disclaimed all responsibility for them.

If he is a democrat of the liberal persuasion, he should not take offence at the use by the hero of the slogan, A nous la liberté! : it is a cry of distress, even despair, which he utters to disguise the misery of his exile.

As I sped along that reddish track, the thought of my father continued to plague me. Had he already returned home? I was hoping he might still be away, but at the same time (knowing his habits well) something told me that he was almost certainly back. No hope on that score, then. At the thought of our impending encounter, my initial feeling of cold terror was soon replaced by a kind of anticipatory excitement. I can't really explain this phenomenon : it was rather like a young toreador going into the ring to meet his first bull, and hearing the preliminary yells of the *aficionados*.

My father. H'm. When he found out everything that had been going on in Kala, he would fairly spit fire, like the phoney old dragon he was. Well, if he was going to spit fire, it'd be more to my advantage to retaliate in kind. What did he expect me to do? Confess All from the word go, weep at his feet and beg his forgiveness? At this a bitter taste came into my mouth, as though I had vomited bile. It was not exactly rebellion as yet, properly speaking, so much as the warning signals of rebellion. At the time I didn't realize this. But I was beginning to kick my heels up, like a colt that can't bear the restraining authority of the bit.

My father: the words evoked twenty years of almost continual terror. At any moment he was liable to materialize where I least expected him. He was inescapable. And, at once, he would begin an inquisition on my behaviour: what had I been doing, where had I been, had I worked hard at school, were they pleased with me, would I pass my exam? He was like a bloody policeman – no, worse: a private dictator, a domestic tyrant. There was never any peace or sense of security; nothing but rows, reproaches, and fear.

He had packed me off to school as young as he could. My mother had been unwise enough to protest, and this had earned her a formidable dressing-down, poor dear. She said no more; simply formed a silent opposition.

My father had been obsessionally determined that I should get immediate promotion from one class to the next every term, without ever staying put longer. There were endless private confabulations with the masters. 'Please,' he would say, 'punish him as often as he deserves it. Do not be swayed by any regard for my feelings.'

I collected my Primary and Elementary Certificates, and took the first part of the General Certificate. A friend said to my father: 'The boy's been too long at school already. He's got quite enough diplomas – what on earth do you want him to *do* eventually?'

My father replied: 'Well, what would he do at home, anyway? Go to the bad, just like his brother. It's best for him to stay at school.'

My mother often used to say to me: 'He's got some scheme

164

at the back of his head, I'm certain of that: I know him too well. Maybe he wants you to go to Europe or something, but he'd kill me sooner than say.'

Well, I didn't go to Europe – not for that sort of thing, anyway. In fact, as far as my father's concerned, I've gone to the bad all right, just like my elder brother.

And perhaps, you know, there was no particular plan lurking at the back of my father's mind after all; no desire to realize long-lost ambitions through my successes. It may well have been that he was simply following the fashion, and that his naturally violent personality took everything to extremes.

Do you remember that period? Fathers used to take their children to school as they might lead sheep into a slaughterhouse. Tiny tots would turn up from backwood villages thirty or forty miles up-country, shepherded by their parents, to be put on the books of some school, it didn't matter which. They formed a miserable floating population, these kids: lodged with distant relations who happened to live near the school, underfed, scrawny, bullied all day by ignorant monitors. The books in front of them presented a universe which had nothing in common with the one they knew: they battled endlessly with the unknown, astonished and desperate and terrified.

We were those children – it is not easy to forget – and it was our parents who forced this torment upon us. Why did they do it?

We were catechized, confirmed, herded to Communion like a gaggle of holy-minded ducklings, made to confess at Easter and on Trinity Sunday, to march in procession with banners on the Fourteenth of July; we were militarized, shown off proudly to every national and international commission.

That was us. Remember?

Ragged, rowdy, boastful, nit-infested, cowardly, scab-ridden, scrounging little beasts, feet swollen with jiggers: that was us; a tiny squeaking species adrift in the modern age like poultry in mid-Atlantic. What god were we being sacrified to, I wonder?

My father was a real shyster, come to think of it. (When I say 'was' I'm using a figure of speech. My father isn't in fact dead, but he's no more than a shadow of his old self, hardly recognizable as what he once was. In fact, not to mince matters, he's gone gaga.) He was a living example of the astonishing results that can occur when Western hypocrisy and commercial materialism are grafted on to a first-rate African intelligence. Some of these results were quite admirable, some disastrous: but my father was the quintessential Westernized native of one generation back.

Let me give you some instances. My father's original intention was to construct a really magnificent coconut-plantation, the finest for fifty miles around. I personally loathed my father, and have continued to do so to a greater or lesser degree according to my age; but I have never ceased to admire the way in which he brought this enterprise to a successful conclusion – in other words, his *style*. Knowing what a passion all his compatriots have for parties and family gatherings – however little like parties the latter may be – he used to invite all his half-brothers and nephews round once a month, and say to them: 'I'd like you to help me do a little job. There's plenty of wine laid on this morning; so you can wet your whistles before you go out to work, and finish it up when you're done.'

Now I look back on these occasions, I will admit that he was in fact extremely generous to his 'workers': he not only offered them a drop of wine, as he put it, but real feasts both before and after their labours. The thing rapidly became a traditional custom. Every month, the family turned up – each member at least once – and worked for my father, reckoning on the feasting and drinking which would be laid on free at the beginning and end to recompense them for the sweat involved. There was a very sizeable number of half-brothers, nephews, and cousins in the families round about. In this way my father's plantation grew in the twinkling of an eye, and there wasn't any miracle about it, either. It grew till it was the most imposing plantation in the district. At this point certain covetous eyes were turned upon it, and my father's ambitions, as a result, came to an abrupt halt.

This scheme was only one among his brilliant inspirations. There was another, more astonishing still for any honest person – such as you or me. As his plantation grew, so did my father's income. Do you know what he did with his money? You can believe me or not as you please, but he *handed the stuff out*; he gave to anyone who cared to have it – on loan. He took a special interest in the backwoods boys – the country yobs, as we call them in my village. As you know, these people never have any loose cash, and are always after it. Well, suppose a man wanted a thousand francs, my father would cheerfully lend it to him. Of course, the poor fellow never managed to repay when the time came – nor did my father expect that he would. At this point the yob would be sick enough with fright to fall in with anything my father suggested. He was, inevitably, the possessor of a small flock, like all backwoods boys. Very well, my father would say, here was a compromise solution: he could pay in kind. Now we get to the nub of the matter. My father used to value these sheep and goats and whatnot at the absolute minimum price per head. The debtor raised no objection to this practice for the excellent reason that since he never had any real money, he attached an almost superstitious reverence to the smallest coin. It was rather like the practice of our ancestors, who traded their relations for old flint-locks. Anyway, that was how the trick worked.

Having secured all this livestock for a song, my father would cart it off to town on the hoof and resell at a cracking profit. Then the whole cycle could begin all over again. A real shyster, my father, just as I said.

But that wasn't all. As you know, in our village there's always some girl somewhere who belongs to the tribe and wants to leave her husband for one reason or another. It isn't enough for her to get a divorce; she wants her dowry back. Normally any husband who's got his hands on a dowry takes great care to avoid getting mixed up in divorce proceedings, in order to avoid having to repay what he's spent. This was no obstacle with my father around; he would offer to repay the dowry himself, out of sheer brotherly kindness. His kindness was such that the girl thus released – without any explicit request from my father, but by a kind of inspired intuition – would come and spend several days with us, and occupy her time by working in my father's fields, hoeing away at his maize and ground-nuts.

Such were the recollections and impressions of my father that whirled madly round my head as I rode along, bouncing up and down on my bicycle like a jumping-jack.

A mile or two from home I noticed a hut with a familiar kind of bottle on its veranda. I stopped, left my bike in the ditch beside the road, and went over to investigate. I had a little money left over which I hadn't spent at college. It was a wine-shop, all right.

I asked for a litre of palm-wine and, to my great astonishment, knocked it straight back.

'Same again,' I said.

The man gave it to me, and remarked: 'Lucky the young folks are still drinking palm-wine; we'd be out of a job if it wasn't for them. You can't get the old chaps to touch anything but that red muck these days. You know, I often wonder, if the white men pulled out – and it doesn't seem impossible – where would these old geysers get their red wine from after that?'

There was a pause. Then, noticing that I was still drinking greedily, he added: 'Hot today, isn't it?'

'Oh, that's not why I'm drinking,' I said. 'In point of fact I'm not particularly thirsty, even.'

'Well, why *are* you drinking, then?'

'To keep my courage up.'

'Ah,' he said, 'you've got something there. There's nothing like good old palm-wine for keeping funk in its place. Our ancestors knew that. I suppose he's bigger than you, eh?'

'Who?'

'The chap you're going to have a row with.'

'Oh, him. Well, honestly, I don't know. That's just why I'm drinking. *Because I don't know.*'

'What's he done to you,' the man inquired, 'pinched your wife?'

'No, no,' I said, somewhat taken aback. 'But, well, it's just the same as if he had. Exactly the same, actually, because I've got a feeling that's just what he's *going* to do.'

He stared at me with some interest. 'Where are you from, might I ask?' he inquired. His tone was half-kindly, half-suspicious.

'Don't you recognize me? I know you – your name's —'

He jumped. 'Lord, I've got it! You're Jean-Marie Medza, aren't you? The son of old Medza, the chap who's always going round the country collecting the cash people owe him. I suppose that's what he lives on, calling in loans – everybody seems to have borrowed some off him at some time. He's a tough creditor, your old man is. Nothing personal against you mind – but, between ourselves —'

'It's all right, old chap,' I said; 'don't worry about *my* feelings.'

'Well, well, so it's you. My God, how you've grown! Still at school, are you? Must be tired of it, after all the time you've been there. I remember when you first went; you were so small you hardly came up to my knee. Don't you find school an awful strain?'

After polishing off the second bottle of wine I left. I felt in a nicely aggressive mood; I was no longer afraid of my father. I was in a great mood, ready to be as rude as hell at the drop of a hat, and whistling nonchalantly to establish my reputation as a devil-may-care.

I got home early in the afternoon. My father was back, shut up in his private room as usual at this time of day, not speaking to anyone. My mother, too, was at home: I heard her talking in the kitchen. As usual, she was scolding my younger sister for some childish crime or other. In our house scolding was the order of the day. My father scolded everyone, and my mother scolded the children – all except the eldest, and there was a good reason for this exception: the boy was hardly ever at home. When he did turn up, there was no question of being cross with him; one harsh word and he would vanish again. When it came to the children themselves, the boys took it out on the girls, and the elder sister told off the younger. (At the time of which I write my elder sister had just got married, so she was no longer about the house; but she had gone on scolding her younger sister right up to the eve of her wedding, thus maintaining family tradition.) Everyone scolded and thrashed everyone else, everyone had their preordained victim; and it was the head of the household who set the example that they all followed.

I propped my large, flashy bicycle against the low balustrade of the veranda and went in. My father appeared, but hardly vouchsafed me a glance. He asked me no questions, and I said nothing to him: a generally cordial atmosphere reigned. I kept on whistling compulsively, although I knew it was a habit he detested, and without allowing for the fact that it attracted snakes. My father had a cold horror of snakes – a horror which I have inherited. I wandered round the house, whistling all the time, like a monarch surveying his kingdom, or a colonial official in Senegal, or even Buffalo Bill in Oklahoma. My father, his face screwed up in concentration, looked exactly as though he were staring clean through the midday sun in order to make out some extraordinary mythical object behind it.

Next, I called my younger sister, in ringingly authoritative tones which made my father jump half out of his skin. I was gradually abandoning my self-control more and more, deliberately trying to provoke him into speaking to me. But it was no good; there he sat in a chair by the window, one elbow leaning on the sill, lost in contemplation of the sun. I kept watching him out of the corner of my eye. He was surprisingly youthful still, and I was sorry to have to treat him as an enemy when we should have been close friends. My younger sister came in, as nervously abrupt as ever, and said, in some astonishment: 'So you're back, are you?'

She was my favourite sister, and had always been very decent to me; but this was no time for cosy amiability. I answered waspishly: 'What a stupid question! You know damn well I'm back the minute you see me.'

'Have you brought *her* with you?'

'Ah, for God's sake: does it look like it?'

I pointed to my canvas shoes, dusty, blackened, and filthy. She understood at once; she took the shoes and went out, with a quick ironic glance at my father *en passant*.

I took another few turns up and down the room, still whistling with depressing persistence. It was my father's house, and my father was present. He made no kind of reaction to my behaviour. Tiring of this little game, I went out to the kitchen, where the women were, and told them the story of my travels. My mother listened with half an ear only, as though she had something else on her mind. When I had finished my little monologue, Aunt Amou remarked merely how much I had changed. 'Very, very odd,' she said. 'You're almost a different person.'

'How have I changed?' I inquired.

'I couldn't exactly say. You're simply *not yourself*; it's as though you were another boy altogether who happened to be your physical double —'

Obviously, then, they hadn't got wind of all the goings-on at Kala. At this point my mother said: 'Your father's very angry because you failed your exam.'

'No kidding?' I said, with carefully assumed lack of concern. 'Is he still on about *that*?'

My sister giggled and said: 'I think he's going to give you a good thrashing.'

'Thrash *me*? Don't be daft.'

'It's no joke,' my sister said. 'I saw him getting the rubber strap out.'

In the normal way my father thrashed his children with flywhisks, and his wife with a thin, whippy cane which looked like a snake and stung just as hard. He only used the rubber strap on really serious occasions, for what might be described as exemplary punishments. This rubber strap was a long strip cut from a car-tyre. It didn't look as if it could do you much damage; it never drew blood or lacerated the skin as the fly-whisks or the cane did. But the day after you had been beaten with it, you found yourself, surprisingly, a mass of aches and sprains and purple bruises, all swollen and lumpy.

Suddenly I knew that my father would never beat me again; that if he pushed me to the limit, there was only one possible result – a fight. As you will have seen, it took me many years to make this simple discovery.

For about a week my relations with my father were virtually non-existent – on the surface, at any rate. Underneath, things were building up to a climax: the powder-train was laid, and it needed only a tiny spark to touch it off.

My tactics remained more or less constant. I went whistling round the house, interrupting my sister rudely on the slightest provocation, and talking in a loud voice. Despite all this, my father took not the slightest notice; he never addressed a single word to me. When I came in, he went out. If I spoke, he remained silent. There was another queer and unexpected result to all this guerrilla warfare: he changed his meal-times. When the hour at which he normally ate was approaching, he would go off for a walk, anywhere, simply to avoid sitting at the same table as me.

I took to keeping a daily journal in which I noted down every detail of my father's behaviour. I set about analysing him as a case-history. I use the word advisedly; as the result of some smattering of psychology which I had picked up at college, I had come to the conclusion that my father would be better off in a psychiatric clinic or even possibly an asylum than in his own home. One evening, somewhat to my own surprise, I jotted down the clinical term *fugue* on a page of my notebook. It struck me that his present behaviour betrayed a typical fugal pattern. What was the explanation? Had this tendency been set up by some new element in my personality? Was my aunt right when she told me I had completely changed? Had I in fact just passed through one of those crises essential to growing up, to acquiring adult status? Whatever the reason, I was cock-a-hoop at the idea that my father actually felt compelled to go into mental retreat on my account.

Besides this, I was drinking heavily. The villagers refused to give me wine, fearing my father's reprisals if he caught them; so I used to go three or four miles up the road, half-way between our village and the little town of Vimili. We had relatives here, and they made no difficulties about letting me have all I wanted to drink. My emancipation thus proceeded at a remarkable rate. When I had a good load aboard I would trudge heavily home.

My mother was in a permanent state of misery. With an intuitive sense the basis of which I had never fathomed, she kept saying that something dreadful was going to happen, she felt it in her bones, that my father and I couldn't go on like this. She tried to get me to go and apologize to my father.

'Apologize for what?' I asked.

'Oh, I don't know – everything, I suppose: failing the exam., being insolent —'

But, quite seriously, I was damned if I would apologize for my exam result to a single living being; it was simply inconceivable.

I often dreamed of Edima, but they were very odd dreams now. It was as though she had become an unattainable object, like some small fish which nibbles at your hook for a moment and then pulls free into the river once more. When that happens you know in your heart that you'll never get a chance to catch that one again. That was the kind of dream I had about her. I loved her as much as ever – more than ever, in fact – but I failed to see how Edima and I could live together in such a tense, explosive family atmosphere.

Up till now my father had been at great pains to ensure that I had no sexual experience whatsoever. (He was convinced that my elder brother's early and complete divergence from the straight and narrow path was to be blamed on women:

cherchez la femme, as they say.) He had given me such enormous complexes on the subject that the mere notion of making love to Edima in the same house where he was sleeping was enough to turn me completely impotent.

If he were to change his tack and become more friendly, it was just conceivable that, given time, my complexes might fade and vanish. But as things were at the moment that seemed a remote chance. A few days spent away from Edima, in the bosom of my family, had been enough to cast me back to the depths of the abyss, where possible and impossible were fatally confused. Every sort of plan passed through my mind: notably that of taking Edima away as soon as she arrived. But where could I take her *to*? I had neither money, help, or experience.

I was weary and sick of the whole dreary business; and finally I made up my mind to rebuild my life without Edima. As soon as I had made up my mind about this, I felt absolutely desolate. I went through hours of the most appalling suffering without being able to unburden my feelings. There was no one I could turn to who would understand my dilemma in the faintest degree.

The evening before Edima was due to arrive, I could think of nothing better to do than run away. I didn't actually leave the house with this idea in mind; I thought I was just going to slip out and pay a call on those relations of mine for an extra bottle or two, as I was in the habit of doing. But once there, I stayed, probably out of plain funk. The whole business had become too complicated for me. My poor nerves and overtaxed brain had never been adequately prepared to cope with this kind of emotional crisis. Echoes of the delegation's arrival reached me there, plain and unequivocal: there was talk of a vast flock of sheep, and much envy expressed for 'good old Medza', thus elevated into the role of Fortune's favourite. Meanwhile I tried to picture my father's expression when faced with a totally unexpected bridal delegation. Luckily, my uncle would be there to explain the situation, and maybe damp down his fury a bit, supposing this to be possible.

I stayed with these obliging relatives for two days, unable to make up my mind what to do. But on the morning of the third day I drank a good deal more than I should have done. In this state of advanced intoxication I couldn't resist the urge to see Edima again, to touch her and hear her voice and feel her breath caressing my chin. I promptly set off home, though my hosts, with an eye to my present condition, did everything they could to dissuade me. After a four-mile walk, and what with the fear and mental agony I now felt inside me, I had sobered up quite a bit by the time I got there.

I made a noisy entry into the village, singing, whistling, and shouting by turns. I found my father standing on the veranda of our bungalow. On the open ground in front were broken bottles, fragments of food, and other signs of recent festivities. (I found out afterwards that he had been exceedingly polite to the delegation, and delighted by the arrival of little Edima, for whom he at once began making private plans which did not include me.) As no one knew where I had vanished to, the local population – and especially the delegation from Kala – crowded out on their doorsteps when I hove in sight, highly intrigued by my riotous behaviour. I walked past my father, singing the Orphan's Lament that Duckfoot Johnny had taught me. I was just making for the kitchen, peaceably enough, to find Edima, when my father called out to me.

'Hey, you there, where have you been?'

'Do you mind not referring to me as "you there"?' I snapped back.

'Well, well!' he said. 'And how should I refer to you, pray?'

'Anyone interested in such details of etiquette should apply to the local Registry Office. They will show you my birth certificate.'

'The boy's gone raving mad,' said my father.

I went into the kitchen and found my mother, Aunt Amou, and my younger sister in a terrified huddle. Edima was there too, but she hadn't the faintest notion of what all the kuffuffle was about. I gave her a smacking kiss, sat down beside her and clasped her hand in mine; we sat like that, in a kind of daze, for quite a while. Then my cousin came in: I was delighted to see him again. He took me aside and said: 'Your father's in one hell of a temper, boy, really off his rocker. If my own old man hadn't been here he'd have clocked someone good and hard by now. No one could be responsible for his actions at the moment.'

'What about later?' I said.

It wasn't till quite late in the afternoon that the balloon really went up.

First of all we heard snatches of conversation coming from the men's quarters; they went on and on without stopping. Then Zambo and I decided to take a walk and clear the air a bit. As we passed outside my father's window we heard him in full spate.

'I've worn my fingers to the bone for those two boys,' he was shouting. 'How on earth did they both come to turn out such no-goods? You can see the cross I've got to bear for yourself. What's more, my dear brother, do you know why he failed his exams? Shall I tell you? *Women.* I'll wager you he's done nothing but lay women the whole year he's been in the city. He *drinks*, too. He hasn't opened a book since he got back from Kala; he's spent his whole time running around the countryside drinking, or chasing the girls, like a dog on heat. What a worthless son! He could get through his exams next October if he really wanted to, but that's the last thing he's concerned about. If you weren't here, my dear fellow, I can assure you he'd be half-dead by now, I'd have given him such a tanning —'

Exasperated by such a degree of injustice and lack of understanding, humiliated beyond words by this casual threat of corporal punishment – he could hardly have chosen a worse moment – I lost control completely.

'I'm not going to college any more,' I yelled through the window. 'I don't want to take any more exams. Anyone who thinks it's easy ought to go and have a shot at it instead of me! Anyway, I'm through with all this nonsense. I'm not standing for anyone beating me, d'you hear? *No more beatings.* Got it?'

There was a noise of crashing furniture and slamming doors, and my father appeared, waving his rubber strap as though it were a cudgel capable of murdering someone. He looked absolutely livid with fury; but I still felt detached enough to note, in a clinical way, how his anger spoilt the lines of his handsome face. He was hardly across the threshold when my uncle flung himself on him, with the obvious intention of stopping the massacre.

I stood there in the forecourt without budging. My mother came out of her kitchen – that cave where she had taken permanent refuge from her lion of a husband – and begged me, tears in her eyes, to go, and not offend by father any further. Did I want to have his curse on me? she asked. I didn't move.

The two men began a prolonged and energetic struggle, under the amused and critical eyes of Zambo and myself. My father fought with all the fury of a wild beast wounded by the hunter's first shot: all the neighbours came out of their houses to watch. From all sides voices were raised exhorting me to get out while I could. 'What are you waiting for, you young fool? Out of it, quick!' they shouted.

At this moment my father succeeded in breaking the iron grip in which my uncle had held him, and hurled himself at me. I hastily ran over in my mind the few rudiments of boxing I had learnt from my friends in college; but when the moment came, I couldn't bring myself to hit him, and gave ground rapidly. My father swung his great club-like strap aloft, and I dodged in the nick of time: so quickly, in fact, that the strap flew out of his hand, bounced, and ended up at my feet. I grabbed it, and my father flung himself on me, fists clenched. I dodged again, with some agility, and the spectators roared with laughter.

'Well done, cousin!' Zambo yelled delightedly. 'Lovely

footwork!' (This tribute cost him a severe dressing-down afterwards from his own father.)

My mother was now crying her eyes out. My father stood there, out of breath. Panting, he said: 'Declared war on me, have you? All right. We'll see who wins —'

He sprang at me again, and I sprinted off with him hard on my heels. After a moment I saw I was gaining rapidly on him, so I slowed down, watching him the whole time over my shoulder. Just as he caught up with me I put on a sudden tremendous burst of speed, like a Welsh international wing-three-quarter. Then I slowed up again. My father didn't give up for an instant, though his lungs must have been bursting. Heavens, how done in he was! Once more he caught up with me, and this time I didn't break into a sprint but side-stepped quickly to the left. He fell flat on his face.

Some of the men burst out laughing, and all the women began to sob and invoke their dead ancestors, though what relevance this pious activity had to our little contest I can't imagine. My father sprang up in one quick movement, his face a mask of anger. But he was really at the end of his tether by now; and besides, we were supposed to be enjoying our-selves – the party wasn't officially over. So I led him a fine dance, rather the kind of thing one does to a child who's learning to walk. I dodged round people, twisting and turn-ing, weaving about, taking unexpected corners, as elusive as quicksilver. Then my father stopped suddenly, positively foaming at the mouth with rage, and said to the men watch-ing this unequal match: 'Why the hell can't some of you catch him for me? Are you going to let a boy make a public laughing-stock of his own father?'

The old men obviously couldn't run at my speed; the young fellows made a show of chasing me, but their hearts weren't in it, and they let me dodge them on purpose, tripping up and sprawling on the ground as if to say that I was really far too quick and tough for them. Only one of them meant business – a cousin of mine who obviously owed money to my father and was, as everyone knew, heavily in debt. He got a tight grip on my belt, and hammer him as I might in the ribs and wind, he wouldn't let go.

I was already picturing the imminent moment when my father (who was tremendously strong in the arms) would get hold of me and beat me senseless to repay me for the way I had just treated him. Once again I mentally assembled everything I had ever learnt about boxing, much as a commander assembles his decimated regiment for one final desperate assault. But Zambo was quicker than my father. He came up behind the man who had hold of my belt and knocked him out. The men hooted with delight, the women howled louder than ever. That was the occasion on which I realised that for women tears are merely a way of expressing emotions.

Zambo's intervention got him into further trouble with his father, who now began a secondary chase – of Zambo – but without much enthusiasm for the job.

My father gave up and went back to his house, breathing hoarsely and looking like murder. Personally, I don't think he ever really got over this little display. I stood there and watched him go; and at that moment I honestly felt sorry for him.

Then I went towards the house myself, and in an authoritative voice ordered my younger sister to pack my things. After my recent demonstration she was only eager to obey. She was just going into the house when my father roared: 'One step farther, my girl, and see what happens!'

This remark had the most surprising effect on my sister. She jumped back so instinctively and abruptly that she lost her footing and fell flat.

'Ah, the hell with my luggage,' I said to the world at large, and walked away to the road in very leisurely fashion, watched by everybody, including the Kala delegation. I went off in a solemn and dignified fashion, without a single backward glance at my native village. I was leaving, it was all over. I have never returned from that day to this. *A nous la liberté*, I murmured to myself.

At the bend in the road I heard someone calling my name: it was my cousin Zambo. He said: 'Can I come with you? I can't stay alone there with all the old fogies.'

We sought refuge with my mother's brother, who lived nearly twenty miles away. A few weeks later my mother visited me there, and brought my belongings with her. She told me my father had been very odd since I left. He had been less inclined to find fault with people, he hardly spoke at all, and he seemed very miserable. He had treated the Kala delegation exactly as custom demanded, neither more nor less; they had gone back home now, and had left Edima behind in our house. She was still waiting for me to come back every day, absolutely convinced that it was only a question of time. She behaved sensibly, said little, and always had her eyes fixed on the road up which I had vanished. My brother had come back home.

Now although I did, in fact, pass my exams that October, as you know, and got a job, I never went back to find Edima. I quickly realized that she could be nothing more than a passing stage in my life. If I had remained permanently at this stage myself, things would certainly have gone better for me; but the fact was that I didn't, and thenceforward I had to start a new career.

It turned out to be a life of endless wandering: different people, changing ideas, from country to country and place to place. During these peregrinations my cousin Zambo and I stuck together, like two limbs attached to the same body.

What did we do together? We shared the same food and drink, made love to the same women, were imprisoned and tortured together, experienced the same miseries and disillusionments, shared the same joys. He is always there at my side; but he says little, and I never entirely understand him. Above all, I have no idea of what it is he really wants, his elusive goal. My own is that true purity which Edima hinted at, and which, now, I am probably too old ever to find.

. . . . .

Yet I remain proud of my mission to Kala – that mission which formed the original subject of my story, though I must apologize for wandering fairly far afield from it at times. Niam got his wife back, even if he didn't exactly thank me for the privilege. Anyway, which of us, when you come to think of it, really owed thanks to the other?

The more I think about it, the more certain I am that it is I who owe him a debt of gratitude for sending me on a journey which enabled me to discover many truths. Not least among these was the discovery – made by contact with the country folk of Kala, those quintessential caricatures of the 'colonized' African – that the tragedy which our nation is suffering today is that of a man left to his own devices in a world which does not belong to him, which he has not made and does not understand. It is the tragedy of man bereft of any intellectual compass, a man walking blindly through the dark in some hostile city like New York. Who will tell him that he can only cross Fifth Avenue by the pedestrian crossings, or teach him how to interpret the traffic signs? How will he solve the intricacies of a subway map, or know where to change trains?

EPILOGUE

EDIMA is today my brother's wife.

How this came about I cannot be certain, since I have never returned home – and, indeed, never shall till after my father's death, and only then to comfort my poor mother.

I have no notion how Edima and my brother came to love each other – supposing that they do. Probably Edima became weary of waiting for me, and felt in the mood to listen to my brother's gallant proposals: certainly he could never set eyes on a pretty girl without trying to make her. So they probably slept together, an event which my father, the cunning old fox, could be relied on to discover. It must have been at this point that he married them off, whether they wanted it or not. What their feelings were I can't imagine.

All I have managed to find out is that they have three children, two of them boys. My father must be pleased at heart by this; I can hear him saying that even the most worthless scamps can do well enough at stud. I know that besides desiring academic success for his sons he also had an atavistic urge to see his stock spread and multiply, perpetuating itself for the future. People like him always win out in the end, somehow.

That is the end of my story. I have no notion what you will make of it, but I have reached a point at which I have no alternative but to write it down. It obsesses me so completely that at times I even fear I may never find any other theme as long as I live. I am haunted by the story of my love for Edima, which is also the story of my first, perhaps my only, love: the absurdity of life.